Dear Reader,

Great news—in February 2013 Harlequin Presents Extra is merging with Presents so you will now be able to find more of your favorite authors in one place as Presents increases from six books a month to eight.

There will be more of the themes you love, such as secret babies, marriages of convenience, scandalous affairs, all with exciting international settings and delicious alpha heroes.

You can also find some of the authors you have come to know and love from Presents Extra in our new contemporary series Harlequin KISS which is launching in February 2013.

So remember, from February onward there will be eight new Presents books available each month!

Happy reading!

The Presents Editors

P.S. Also available this month:

#229 SECRETS OF CASTILLO DEL ARCO
Bound by his Ring
Trish Morey

#230 MARRIAGE BEHIND THE FAÇADE
Bound by his Ring
Lynn Raye Harris

#231 KEEPING HER UP ALL NIGHT
Temptation on her Doorstep
Anna Cleary

#232 THE DEVIL AND THE DEEP
Temptation on her Doorstep
Amy Andrews

"There is no marriage, Malik. Sign the papers and it's done."

His smile was not quite a smile. "Ah, but it's not so easy as that. I am a Jahfaran prince. There is a protocol to follow."

Sydney reached for the door frame to steady herself. A bad feeling settled into her stomach, making the tension in her body spool tighter and tighter. Her knees felt weak, making her suddenly unstable on her tall designer pumps. "What protocol?"

He speared her with a long look. A pitying look?

By the time he spoke, her nerves were at snapping point.

"We must go to Jahfar—"

"What?"

"—and we must live as man and wife for a period of forty days...."

Dying. She was dying inside. And he was so controlled, as always. "No," she whispered, but he didn't hear—or he didn't care. His eyes were flat, unfeeling.

"Only then can we apply to my brother the King for a divorce."

MARRIAGE BEHIND THE FAÇADE

LYNN RAYE HARRIS

~ Bound by his Ring ~

HARLEQUIN®
entertain, enrich, inspire™

Recycling programs
for this product may
not exist in your area.

ISBN-13: 978-0-373-52898-1

MARRIAGE BEHIND THE FAÇADE

FIRST NORTH AMERICAN PUBLICATION 2013

This edition published by arrangement with Harlequin Books S.A.

For questions and comments about the quality of this book, please contact us at CustomerService@Harlequin.com.

® and TM are trademarks of Harlequin Enterprises Limited or its corporate affiliates. Trademarks indicated with ® are registered in the United States Patent and Trademark Office, the Canadian Trade Marks Office and in other countries.

www.Harlequin.com

Printed in U.S.A.

LYNN RAYE HARRIS read her first Harlequin® romance when her grandmother carted home a box from a yard sale. She didn't know she wanted to be a writer then, but she definitely knew she wanted to marry a sheikh or a prince and live the glamorous life she read about in the pages. Instead, she married a military man and moved around the world. She's been inside the Kremlin, hiked up a Korean mountain, floated on a gondola in Venice and stood inside volcanoes at opposite ends of the world.

These days Lynn lives in North Alabama with her handsome husband and two crazy cats. When she's not writing, she loves to read, shop for antiques, cook gourmet meals and try new wines. She is also an avowed shoeaholic and thinks there's nothing better than a new pair of high heels.

Lynn was a finalist in the 2008 Romance Writers of America's Golden Heart® contest, and she is the winner of the Harlequin® Presents Instant Seduction contest. She loves a hot hero, a heroine with attitude and a happy ending. Writing passionate stories for Harlequin is a dream come true. You can visit her at www.lynnrayeharris.com.

Other titles by Lynn Raye Harris available in ebook:

Harlequin Presents® Extra

Harlequin Presents

CHAPTER ONE

It was done. Sydney Reed dropped the pen and stared at the documents she'd just signed.

Divorce papers.

Her heart hammered in her throat, her palms sweated. Her stomach cramped. She felt as if someone had taken away the last shred of happiness she would ever, ever know.

But that was absurd. Because there was no happiness where Prince Malik ibn Najib Al Dhakir was concerned. There was only heartache and confusion.

Though it irritated her, just thinking his name still had the power to send a shiver tiptoeing down her spine. Her exotic sheikh. Her perfect lover. Her husband.

Ex-husband.

Sydney shoved the papers into the waiting envelope and buzzed her assistant, Zoe. Why was this so hard? It shouldn't be. Malik had never cared for her. She'd been the one who'd felt everything. But it wasn't enough. One person couldn't feel enough emotion for two. No matter how hard she tried, Malik was never going to love her. He simply wasn't capable of it. Though he was a generous and giving lover, his heart never engaged.

Of course it didn't. Sydney frowned. It wasn't that

he *couldn't* love—he just couldn't love *her*. She was not the right woman for him. She never had been.

Zoe appeared in the door, her expression all business.

"Call the courier. I need these delivered right away," Sydney said before she could change her mind.

Zoe didn't even acknowledge the tremble in Sydney's fingers as she handed over the thick sheaf of papers. "Yes, Miss Reed."

Miss Reed. Not Princess Al Dhakir.

Never Princess Al Dhakir again.

Sydney nodded, because she didn't trust herself to speak, and turned back to her computer. The screen was a little blurry, but she resolutely clenched her jaw and got on with the business of selecting property listings to show the new client she was meeting with later.

She'd been such a fool. She'd met Malik over a year ago when someone on his staff had called her parents' real estate firm to arrange for an agent to show him a few properties. She hadn't known who Malik was, but she'd quickly familiarized herself with his background before their appointment.

Prince of Jahfar. Brother to a king. Sheikh of his own territory. Unmarried. Obscenely wealthy. International playboy. Heartbreaker. There had even been a photo of a sobbing actress who claimed she'd fallen in love with Prince Malik, but he'd left her for another woman.

Sydney had gone to the appointment armed with information and, yes, even a dose of disdain for the entitled sheikh who broke hearts so carelessly. Not that she thought he could ever be interested in her. She wasn't glamorous or movie star gorgeous or anything even remotely interesting to a playboy sheikh.

But oh, the joke was on her, wasn't it?

Malik was so charming, so suave. So unlike any man she'd ever met before.

When he'd turned his singular attention on her, she'd been helpless to resist him. She hadn't wanted to resist. She'd been flattered by his interest.

He'd made her feel beautiful, accomplished, special—all the things she definitely was not. A dart of pain lodged beneath her heart. Malik's special gift was making a woman feel as if she were the center of his universe; as long as it lasted, it was bliss.

Her mouth compressing into a grim line, Sydney grabbed the listings from the printer and shoved them into her briefcase. Then she shrugged into the white cotton blazer hanging on the back of her chair. She refused to feel sorry for herself a moment longer. That part of her life was over.

Malik had been happy to be rid of her—and now she was taking the final step and cutting him from her life permanently. She'd half expected him to do it in the year since she'd left him in Paris, but he clearly didn't care enough to make the effort. Whatever the reason, Malik's heart was encased in ice—and she was not the one who could thaw it.

Sydney let Zoe know she was leaving, stopped by her mother's office to say good night and headed out to her car. It took over an hour in traffic to reach the first house in Malibu. She parked in the large circular drive and glanced at her watch. The client would be here in fifteen minutes.

Sydney gripped the steering wheel and forced herself to breathe calmly for a couple of minutes. She felt disjointed, unsettled, but there was nothing she could do about it now. She'd sent the papers; it was the end.

Time to move on.

She went inside the house, turning on lights, opening heavy curtains to reveal the stunning views. She moved as if on autopilot, fluffing the throw pillows on the furniture, spraying cinnamon air freshener and finding a soft jazzy station on the home entertainment system.

Then she walked out onto the terrace and scrolled through the email on her phone while she waited. At precisely seven-thirty, the doorbell rang.

Show time.

She took a deep breath before marching to the door and pasting a giant smile on her face. *Always greet the client with warm enthusiasm.* Her mother's first rule of engagement. Sydney might not be the best salesperson the Reed Team had, but she worked the hardest at it. She had to.

Sydney was the odd duck in the Reed family of swans, the disappointing daughter. The one who made her parents shake their heads and smile politely when what they really wanted to do was ask her why she couldn't be more like her perfect sister.

The only thing she'd ever done that had made them so proud they'd nearly popped was to marry a prince. But she'd failed at that, too, hadn't she? They didn't say anything, but she knew they were disappointed in her.

Sydney pulled the door open, her smile cracking apart the instant her gaze collided with the man's standing on the threshold.

"Hello, Sydney."

For a minute she couldn't move, couldn't speak. Couldn't breathe. She was mesmerized by the dark glitter of those burning, burning eyes. A bird sang in a nearby tree, the sound oddly distorted as all her attention focused on the man standing before her.

The man she hadn't seen, other than in photos in the papers or video clips on television, in over a year.

He was still spectacular, damn him. He was the desert. He was harsh and hard and beautiful. He'd been hers once.

No, he had not. It had been nothing more than an illusion. Malik belonged to no one but himself.

"What are you doing here?" she forced herself to ask.

"Isn't that obvious?" Malik responded, one dark brow lifting sardonically. "I'm looking for a house."

"You have a house," she said inanely. "I sold it to you last year."

"Yes, but I've never liked it."

"Then why did you buy it?" she snapped, her pulse roaring in her veins.

His dark eyes glittered hotly. She almost took a step back, but held her ground beneath the onslaught of his gaze. My God, Malik was all man. There had never been anyone like him in her life. So tall and dark and powerful. Malik walked into a room and owned it. There was never any question who was in charge when Malik was around.

And she had been just as vulnerable to his power as anyone.

He'd *owned* her. He would own her still, had she not realized how destructive a life with him would be. Had she not decided she couldn't give herself so utterly and completely to a man and still mean so little to him.

Pain rolled into a hard knot in her belly.

One corner of his mouth lifted in a grin, though there was no humor in his expression. "I bought it because you wanted me to, *habibti.*"

Sydney's feet were stuck to the floor. Her stomach churned with emotion, and her eyes stung. So much pain and anger in seeing him again. She'd tried to inure herself to his presence in the world by reading every article about him she could find, even when they stabbed her in the heart with tales of his latest conquests. She'd told herself it would only be a matter of time before he returned to L.A. and that if she ran into him again, she would sniff haughtily and act like an ice princess.

And wasn't she doing a fine job of that now?

Sydney stepped away from the door, determined to cloak herself in disdain. She did not need him. She'd never needed him. She'd only thought she had.

Riiight…

Inside, she was a mess. Outside, she was cool. As cool as he was. "And you always do what people want you to do, don't you?" she said.

Malik walked inside and shut the door behind him. "Only if it amuses me."

He took up all the space in the foyer, made it seem far too intimate. She could smell his soap, that special blend he had made in Paris. Her eyes skimmed over him. His suit was custom made, of course. Pale grey. The powder blue shirt beneath his jacket was unbuttoned just enough to show the hollow of his throat.

She knew what that spot tasted like, how it felt beneath her tongue.

Sydney pivoted, moved toward the floor to ceiling windows across the room. Her heart beat triple time. Her pulse throbbed. Her skin felt tight. "Then perhaps it would amuse you to buy a house with such a gorgeous view. I could use the commission."

"If you need money, Sydney, you only have to ask." He sounded so cool, so logical, so detached, as if he were telling his valet that he didn't care whether it was the red tie or the maroon today.

Bitterness flooded her. So typical of him. Nothing engaged Malik's emotions, not really. Her mistake had been in thinking she was different somehow.

Ha. Joke's on you, girlfriend.

She turned back to him. "I don't want your money, Malik. Now why don't you get out before my real client arrives? If you have anything to say to me, you can say it through my lawyer."

The heat in his eyes didn't waver. Her stomach clenched. Was it anger or a different kind of heat she saw there?

"Ah yes, the divorce," he said disdainfully, as if he were talking to a naughty child.

Anger, then. He wasn't accustomed to her fighting back. Because she never had before.

Not until today, when she'd slid her pen across that signature line.

Sydney crossed her arms over her chest. She knew it was a defensive gesture, but she didn't care. "I didn't ask you for anything. Just your signature on those papers."

"So you have signed them finally." There wasn't the least trace of sorrow or surprise in his voice.

Always so calm and cool, her desert lord. It infuriated her that he could be so unaffected.

Her blood felt thick in her veins. Heavy. "Isn't that why you're here?"

It had only been a little over an hour since she'd given the papers to Zoe. It was possible they'd been delivered to Malik in that time—but even if they had, how had he found where she was and gotten here so quickly?

She'd just assumed that was why he'd come. Comprehension unfurled. She felt stupid for not realizing it sooner. He must have known she'd been having the papers drawn up. Though why it mattered to him, she wasn't sure. "There is no client, is there? You set this up."

It was precisely like him to do so. Malik orchestrated things. If he didn't like something, he had it changed. If he wanted something, he got it. He spoke the words, and things happened as if by magic. It was the kind of power that most people would never possess.

He inclined his head. "It seemed the best way to meet with you. Less likely to cause a scene for the paparazzi."

Hot anger threated to scorch her from the inside out. And something else as well. Something hot and dark and secret. Something she recalled from the sultry nights with him, the hours spent tangled together in silken sheets, his body entwining with hers, thrusting into hers, caressing hers.

Why could she never look at this man without thinking of it?

It was the one place where he'd been raw and open with her—or so she'd thought. She knew better now.

Sydney closed her eyes, swallowed. Her skin was moist with perspiration, so she went to the terrace doors, flinging them open to let in the clean ocean breeze. It was always too hot when Malik was near.

She didn't have to turn to know he was right behind her. He vibrated with an energy that she'd never been able to ignore. When Malik walked into a room, she knew it. The hairs on the back of her neck prickled. Her blood hummed. Part of her wanted to turn and go into his arms, wanted to feel the extraordinary bliss of a night in his bed at least one more time.

She despised that part of herself. She wasn't that weak anymore, damn it! She was strong, capable of resisting the animal part of her that wanted this man without reason. Without sense.

But she had to resist—or pay the price.

Sydney whirled, taking a step back when she realized he was closer than she'd thought. "You never bothered to get in touch with me," she said, her voice cracking in spite of her determination. "You let all these months go by, and you never once tried to contact me. So why are you here now?"

His eyes flashed, his lean jaw hardening. He was so very, very beautiful. It wasn't an incongruous word when applied to a man who looked like Malik did. Jet dark hair, chiseled features, honed body, bronzed skin that looked as if he'd been dusted in gold. The most sensuous lips God had ever created. Lips that knew how to bring her to the brink of screaming pleasure again and again.

A tiny shiver crawled down her spine. She should have known a man like him could never truly be interested in her.

"Why would I chase you down, Sydney?" he demanded, ignoring her question. "You chose to leave. You could have chosen to come back."

She drew herself up. Of course he would think that way! Because he hadn't been affected by her going. "I had no choice."

Malik snorted. "Really? Someone made you walk out on our marriage? Someone forced you to run from Paris in the middle of the night with one suitcase and a note left on the counter? I'd like to meet this someone with such power over you."

She stiffened. He made her sound so ridiculous. So childish. "Don't pretend you were devastated by it. We both know the truth."

He brushed past her to stand in the open door and look at the ocean while her heart died just a little with each passing second as she hoped, ridiculously, that he might contradict her.

Why did a small part of her always insist on that rosy naiveté where he was concerned?

"Of course not," he stated matter-of-factly. Then he turned and speared her with an angry look, his voice turning harsh. "But I am an Al Dhakir and you are my *wife*. Did you not consider for one moment the embarrassment this would cause me? Would cause my family?"

Anger and disappointment simmered together in her belly. She'd hoped he might have missed her just a little bit, but of course he had not. Malik didn't need anyone or anything. He was a force of nature all his own.

She'd never understood him. That was only part of the problem between them, but it was a big part. He'd been everything exotic and wonderful and he'd swept her off her feet.

She still remembered the moment she'd realized she was in love with him. And she'd thought he must feel the same since she was the only woman he'd ever wanted to marry.

How wrong she'd been. It hadn't taken very long for her naive hopes to be ground to bits beneath his custom soles. Her eyes filled with angry tears, but she refused to let them fall. She'd had a year to analyze her actions and berate herself for not demanding more from him.

From *life*.

"That's why you're here? Because *you're* embarrassed?" Sydney drew in a trembling breath. Adrenaline surged in her blood, but she was determined to maintain her cool. "My, my, it certainly took you a long time to get worked up."

He took a step toward her. Sydney thrust her chin

out, uncowed. Abruptly, he stopped and shoved his hands into his pockets. The haughty prince assumed control once more as he looked down his refined nose at her. "We could live apart, Sydney. That is practically expected, though usually after there is an heir or two. But divorce is another thing altogether."

"So you're embarrassed about the divorce, not about me leaving," she stated. As if she would ever consider having children with him. So he could leave her to raise the kids while he dallied with mistresses?

No way. She'd been such a fool to think their lives could be normal when they came from such diverse backgrounds. He was a prince of the desert. She was plain Sydney Reed from Santa Monica, California. It was laughable how deluded she had been.

"I've let you have your space," he continued. "But enough is enough."

Sydney felt her eyes widening. A bubble of anger popped, sending fresh heat rushing through her. "You *let* me have my space? What the hell is that supposed to mean?"

His eyes flashed. "Is that any way for a princess to talk?"

"I'm not a princess, Malik." Though technically his wife *was* a princess, she'd never felt like one, even when she'd still been happily married to him. He'd never taken her to Jahfar; she'd never seen his homeland or been welcomed by his family.

She'd never even *met* his family.

That should have been her first clue.

Shame flooded her, made her skin hot once more. How naive she'd been. When he'd married her, she'd thought he'd loved her. She'd had no idea she was simply an instrument of his rebellion. He'd married her because she'd been unsuitable, no other reason. He'd *wanted* to shock his family.

She'd simply been the flavor of the moment, the woman warming his bed when the idea occurred to him.

"You are still my wife, Sydney," he growled. "Until such time as you are not, you will act with the decorum your position deserves."

Sydney's stomach was doing flips. She clenched her fists at her sides, willing herself not to explode. What good would it do?

"Not for much longer, Malik. Sign the papers and you won't have to worry about me embarrassing you ever again." Or that she wasn't good enough for his family's refined taste.

He closed the distance between them slowly…so slowly that she felt as if she were being hunted. Her instinct was to escape, but she refused to give him the satisfaction. She stood her ground as the ocean crashed on the beach outside, as her heartbeat swelled to a crescendo, as he came so close she could smell the scent of his skin, could feel his breath on her face.

His fingers snaked along her jaw, so lightly she might have imagined it. His eyes were hooded, his expression unreadable. She fought the desire to close her eyes, to tilt her face up to his. To feel his lips on hers once more.

She was not that desperate. Not that stupid.

She'd learned. She might have been blindly, ignorantly in love with him once—but she knew better now.

His voice was a deep rumble, an exotic siren call. "You still want me, Sydney."

"I don't." She said it firmly, coldly. Her legs trembled beneath her, her nerve endings shivering with anticipation. Her heart would beat right out of her chest if he kept touching her.

But she would not tell him to stop. Because she would not admit she was affected.

"I don't believe you," he said.

And then his head dipped, his mouth fitting over hers. For a moment she softened; for a moment she let his lips press against hers. For a moment, she was lost in time, flung back to another day, another house, another kiss.

An arrow of pain shot through her breastbone, lodged somewhere in the vicinity of her heart. Was she always destined to hurt because of him?

Sydney pressed her hands against the expensive fabric of his jacket, clenched her fingers in his lapels—and then pushed hard.

Malik stepped back, breaking the brief kiss. His nostrils flared. His face was a set of sharp angles and chiseled features, the waning light from the sunset hollowing out his cheeks, making him seem harder and harsher than she remembered.

Sadder, in a way.

Except that Malik wasn't sad. How could he be? He didn't care about her. Never had. She'd been convenient, a means to an end. Impressionable and fresh in a way his usual women had not been.

The slow burn of embarrassment was still a hot fire inside, even after a year. She'd been so thoroughly duped by his charm.

"You never used to push me away," he said bemusedly.

"I never thought I needed to," she responded.

"And now you do."

"Don't I? What's the point, Malik? Do you wish to prove your mastery over me one last time? Prove that you're still irresistible?"

He tilted his head to one side. "Am I irresistible?"

"Hardly."

"That's too bad," he said.

"Not for me, it isn't." Her head was beginning to throb from too much adrenaline, too much anger.

He pushed a hand through his hair. "It changes nothing," he said. "Though it might make it more difficult."

Sydney blinked. "Make what more difficult?"

"Our marriage, *habibti*."

He was a cruel, cruel man. "There is no marriage, Malik. Sign the papers and it's done."

His smile was not quite a smile. "Ah, but it's not so easy as that. I am a Jahfaran prince. There is a protocol to follow."

Sydney reached for the door frame to steady herself. A bad feeling settled into her stomach, making the tension in her body spool tighter and tighter. Her knees felt weak, making her suddenly unstable on her tall designer pumps. "What protocol?"

He speared her with a long look. A pitying look?

By the time he spoke, her nerves were at the snapping point.

"We must go to Jahfar—"

"What?"

"And we must live as man and wife for a period of forty days…"

Dying. She was dying inside. And he was so controlled, as always. "No," she whispered, but he didn't hear—or he didn't care. His eyes were flat, unfeeling.

"Only then can we apply to my brother the king for a divorce."

CHAPTER TWO

SYDNEY slipped out the door and sank heavily onto a nearby deck chair. Beyond, the Pacific Ocean rolled relentlessly to shore. The surf roiled and foamed, the sound a muted roar as the power of the water hit the beach.

That was Malik's power, she thought wildly. The power to rush over her, to drag her with him, to obliterate what she wanted. That had been part of the reason she'd left, because she'd somehow let her sense of self be pulled under the wave that was Malik. It had frightened her.

That and hearing what his true feelings for her had been. Sydney shuddered.

Finally, she pulled her gaze from the water, which was now turning orange with the sun's setting rays. Malik stood beside her chair. His jaw seemed hard in the waning light, as if he, too, were trapped and trying to make the best of it.

"Tell me it's a joke," she finally said, squeezing her hands together over her stomach.

His gaze flickered to her. His handsome face was so serious, so stark. Even now she felt a twinge of something, some deep feeling, as she looked at him. She refused to examine what that feeling might be; she simply didn't want to know. She wanted to be done with him, finished.

Forever.

"It is not a joke. I am bound by Jahfaran law."

"But we weren't married there!" She laughed wildly. "I've never even *seen* Jahfar, except on a map. How can I possibly be bound by some crazy foreign law?"

He stiffened, but she didn't really care if she'd insulted him. How dare he show up here after all this time and tell her they would remain married until she lived with him for forty days—in the desert, no less! It was like something only Hollywood could think up.

The irony made her laugh. Malik looked at her curiously, but didn't seem to mistake the laugh for real humor. At least he could tell that much. Maybe forty days wouldn't be so bad after all.

Who was she kidding?

"I won't do it," she said, drawing in a deep breath heavy with salt and sea. "I'm not bound by Jahfaran law. Sign the papers and as far as I'm concerned, we're through."

He shifted beside her chair. "You might think it's that easy, but I assure you it is not. You married a foreign prince, *habibti*."

"We were married in Paris." Quickly, by an official at the Jahfaran embassy. As if Malik were afraid he might change his mind if it didn't happen fast. Bitterness ate at her.

That was precisely what he'd been thinking.

"Where we were married matters not," Malik said in that smooth, deep voice of his that still had the power to make her shudder deep inside. "But it does matter by *whom*. We were married under Jahfaran law, Sydney. If you ever wish to be free of me, you will come to Jahfar and follow the protocol."

Sydney tilted her head up to look at him. He was gazing down at her, his expression indecipherable. Anger surged in her veins. "Surely we can find a way to fake it. Your brother is the king!"

"Which is precisely *why* we cannot fake it, as you so charmingly say. My brother takes his duty as king very seriously. He will hold me to the letter of the law. If you wish to be divorced, you will do this."

Sydney closed her eyes and leaned back against the cushion. Dear God. It was a nightmare. A giant, ironic joke from the cosmos. She'd married Malik hurriedly, secretly. There'd been no royal wedding, no fairy tale day with music and beautiful clothes and pageantry.

There'd been the two of them in a registry office at the embassy. A fawning official who called Malik *Your Royal Highness* and bowed a lot. A wide-eyed woman, Sydney remembered, who'd registered the marriage and asked them to sign.

She'd almost felt as if it weren't real, but then the newspapers had picked up on it and suddenly she and Malik were splashed across the tabloids. The attention hadn't died by the time she'd left. And then it followed her back to L.A., finally disappearing a few weeks later when she'd refused to talk to anyone.

Oh, she knew her picture had appeared a few times over the last year, but the paparazzi were far more interested in Malik than they were in her. He was the news. She was a casualty.

And not even a very interesting one.

The last thing she wanted was to remain tied to him, to have the media take a renewed interest in her down the road because Malik caused an international stir of some sort and they wanted to know how his poor wife was handling it. Or, worse, what happened when Malik found someone else he wanted to marry, and he needed her to go to Jahfar for a divorce when he had a current lover in tow?

No. Way. In. Hell.

"Fine," Sydney sniffed. "If that's what it takes, I'll go."

A shiver dripped into her veins. She could get through forty days, if that's what it took to officially end this. Because there was nothing left between them, no danger to her heart any longer. The damage had already been done. There was an iron cage where her heart had once been.

"We can leave tonight. My plane is ready."

Goose bumps crawled across her skin. What had she just agreed to? Panic spread inside until she was quivering with it. "I can't be ready that fast. I need time to put things in order."

The last time she'd dashed off with Malik she'd left her life in disarray. This time, she was putting everything in order before going anywhere. Because this time she would be stepping back into her life without the pain and disorientation of last time.

She'd gone without much thought, because he'd asked her to, and then when he'd asked her to stay, to marry him, she'd impulsively agreed. She'd given no thought to her life back in Los Angeles. A fact that her family never mentioned, but that she knew was very much on their minds whenever they looked at her. She was the impulsive one, the artistic one—the one who could leap without looking but then paid the price later.

And what a price it had been. She'd been a wreck. She'd asked herself in the early days after her return home if she'd been too hasty, if she should have stayed and confronted him, but she always came back to the same thing: Malik regretted marrying her. He'd said so. What was there left to say after that?

She might have loved him, but she would not be anyone's cross to bear. And she'd definitely felt like a burden in the week after his confession. He'd changed, and she simply hadn't been able to take it anymore. She'd never thought a year would pass without any contact between them, but that had only proven he did not want her in his life any longer.

"How much time do you need?" he asked, his voice tight.

"At least a week," she answered automatically, though in fact she knew no such thing. But she wanted to be in control this time. Needed to be in control. It wasn't much, but it was something.

"Impossible. Two days."

Sydney bristled. "Really? Is there a timeline, Malik? A celestial clock somewhere that insists we must do this on a specific timetable? I need a week. I have to make arrangements at work."

And she had to check with her lawyer, just in case she could find some sort of legal loophole that would change everything.

Malik gazed down at her, his dark eyes gleaming hotly. Intensely. She waited almost breathlessly for his answer. Malik was proud, haughty. Aristocratic and used to getting his way. If only she'd told him no when he'd suggested she marry him—but it had never crossed her mind. She'd been too awestruck, and far too much in love with the man she'd thought he was.

Though it was a little late, she would not blindly accept his decrees ever again.

"Fine," he said, his voice clipped. "One week."

Sydney nodded her agreement, her heart pounding as if she'd just run a marathon. "Very well. One week then."

He turned to gaze out at the ocean again. Then he nodded. "I'll take it."

She blinked. "Take what?"

"The house."

"You haven't really seen it," she exclaimed. It was a gorgeous house, one that she only wished she could afford in her wildest dreams, with spacious rooms and breathtaking ocean views. It was the kind of house where she could be inspired to paint, she thought wistfully.

But Malik had only seen the exterior, the main living space, and this terrace. For all he knew, the bedrooms were tiny closets, the bathrooms a 1970s throwback with mustard and orange tiles and psychedelic black fixtures.

Malik shrugged. "It is a house. With a view. It will do."

Inexplicably, a current of anger uncoiled inside her. He was careless when he wanted something. Accustomed to getting whatever he wanted when he wanted it.

Like *her*.

In Malik's world, there were no consequences. No price to be paid when things didn't work out the way you expected. There was only the next house, the next deal.

The next woman.

Dark anger pumped into her. "I'm afraid that's impossible," she said. "There's already an offer."

Malik was unfazed. "Add twenty-five percent. The owner will not turn that kind of money down."

"I think they've already accepted the offer," she

said primly. But guilt swelled inside her as soon as she voiced the lie. The owners were entitled to the sale. Her anger at Malik was no excuse to deprive them of it. "But if you'll give me a moment, I can call and see if there's a chance."

Malik's dark eyes burned into her. "Do it."

Sydney turned away and walked across the terrace. She called the listing broker just to make sure there were no offers, and then strolled back to Malik when she finished. "Good news," she said, though it galled her to do so. "If you can come up half a million, the property is yours."

Because he was too smug, too careless, and she couldn't let him ride roughshod over her. It was a rebellion of a sort to jack up the price. She refused to feel guilty. In fact, she would donate her portion of the commission to charity. At least Malik's money could do someone some good.

"Fine," he murmured. "Whatever it requires."

Bitterness swelled in her veins. "And will you be happy here, Malik? Or will you regret this purchase, too?"

She didn't say what she was really thinking—that he regretted her—but it was implied.

"I never regret my actions, *habibti*. If I change my mind later, I will simply get rid of the property."

"Of course," she said stiffly, shame pounding through her. "Because that is easiest."

Malik could discard whatever he wanted, whatever he no longer needed or desired. He'd spent a lifetime doing so.

His expression didn't change. He looked so haughty, so superior. "Precisely. You will write up the papers, yes?"

"Of course."

"Get them now and I will sign them."

"You don't want to read them first?"

He shrugged. "Why?"

"What if I increase the price another million?"

"Then I would pay it," he said.

Sydney opened her briefcase and jerked a blank offer form from inside. As much as she despised him in that moment, as much as she despised his arrogance and nonchalance, she couldn't succumb to the temptation to take him for a spectacular ride. She quickly wrote in the price, and then shoved the papers at him.

"Sign here," she said, pointing.

He did so without hesitation. She couldn't decide if he was simply arrogant and uncaring or stupidly trusting. A split second later he looked up at her, his eyes sharp and hard, and she knew that stupidly trusting was not the correct choice.

This man not only knew what the fair market price of the property was, he also knew that she'd inflated the price—and he was willing to pay it.

"One week, Sydney," he said, his voice sending a shiver through her body. "And then you are mine."

"Hardly, Your Highness," she said, though her voice shook in spite of her determination not to let it. "It's simply another business arrangement. Forty days in Jahfar in exchange for a lifetime of freedom."

He bowed his head in acknowledgment. "Of course," he said. "You are quite correct."

And yet, as he walked out and left her standing alone with the ocean crashing in the background, she had the sinking feeling that everything about this arrange-

ment was going to be far more complicated than she
wanted it to be.

At least for her…

CHAPTER THREE

It took a week and half to get her life organized, and then to board a flight for Jahfar. Malik was not happy, as his messages indicated more than once, but Sydney refused to feel a moment's worry about it. After he'd left her in the Malibu home—*his* Malibu home now—she'd quickly phoned her lawyer.

Jillian had tried to help, but in the end there was nothing she could do. An American divorce wouldn't do the trick. When she'd originally drawn up the papers, she'd warned Sydney it might not be enough. Sydney had just hoped against hope that it would be. Even if it hadn't been, she hadn't expected an archaic law like the one mandating she live with Malik in Jahfar for forty days.

Forty days. My God.

Sydney sipped the champagne a flight attendant had brought for her. Her first class seat was comfortable, though the flight was full and she certainly wasn't alone. She could have flown on Malik's private plane, but she'd chosen to fly commercial instead. He'd been furious, but she'd held fast to her determination to do so. In the end, he'd gone to Jahfar a few days ahead of her.

Her stomach tightened nervously, and she took another sip of the champagne.

Jahfar. What would she find when she arrived? What would she feel?

It was Malik's home, and she would in some ways be at his mercy. But she was determined to maintain as much control over her life as possible, which was why she'd insisted on making her own arrangements. Yes, it would have been easier to fly with Malik and let him take care of everything.

But she refused to give him that much control.

The plane touched down in Jahfar a couple of hours after dawn. The moment they taxied to the gate, Sydney realized how foolish her thoughts had been. Because nothing was under her control any longer. A flight attendant hurried to her side, hands clutched together in front of her body. The woman seemed nervous, afraid. And then she bowed deeply.

A heavy feeling settled in the pit of Sydney's stomach.

"Princess Al Dhakir, please forgive us for not realizing you were aboard."

"I…" Sydney blinked, her skin heating with embarrassment. "No, that's fine," she said, recovering herself though her heart throbbed painfully. "I didn't wish it to be known."

She felt so pretentious, but what else could she say? There was no explaining, no telling these people not to refer to her as a princess. They wouldn't understand.

The woman bowed again before a man came forward and collected Sydney's carry-on bag from the overhead compartment. Everyone else remained seated as she exited the plane first, her cheeks burning hot. She had an overwhelming urge to strangle Malik when next she saw him.

Which proved to be far sooner than she expected.

The international airport in Port Jahfar teemed with people clothed in both Jahfaran and Western dress, but they fell away like water from a ship's bow as a man and his entourage cleaved through them. The man was tall, dressed in the flowing white *dishdasha* and traditional headdress of Jahfar. At his waist was a curved dagger with a jeweled hilt—surprising in an airport, and yet not so much considering where they were.

And who he was. She realized with a shock that the magnificent man in traditional clothing was actually her husband. Heat softened her bones, flooded her core. She'd never seen Malik in Jahfaran clothing. The effect was…extraordinary.

He was every inch a sheikh. Exotic, dark, handsome. Magnificent.

Malik strode toward her with that arrogant gait of his, his dark eyes burning into her from afar so that she felt the urge to shrink inside herself and disappear. She looked like hell—felt like hell—after so many hours in the air.

And he was like something out of a fairy tale.

Oh, if only she could turn time back an hour or so and change clothes, fix her hair, her makeup.

Why, Sydney? What would be the point in that?

Malik might have made love to her again and again over the two months they were together, but he'd clearly been slumming for his own purposes. Supermodels and beauty queens were more to his taste.

Sydney thrust her chin out. She would not cower or hide. She would not be ashamed.

There was nothing to be ashamed of.

Malik came to a halt before her, his entourage carefully surrounding them both, protecting them, without coming too close.

Her throat felt as dry as sand as his gaze slid over her. "Here I am," she said somewhat inanely. "As promised."

Immediately, she wished she hadn't been the first to speak. It was as if she'd given away some slice of invisible ground in their war with each other, as if she'd arrayed her forces on this particular field of battle and then failed because of something so obvious such as not arming them with weapons.

But it was because of him, because he was making her nervous as he studied her. No doubt he was regretting his impulse to inform anyone she was his wife. She was too casual in her white cotton tank, navy jacket, jeans and ballet flats. A princess should look more polished, like a movie star. She should be sporting Louboutins on her feet, carrying an Yves St. Laurent handbag and wearing the latest Milan fashions.

Well, she wasn't truly a princess and there was little point in pretending to be one for the next month and ten days.

One dark eyebrow arched as he studied her. "Yes, here you are."

Sydney's heart skipped several beats at once, making her feel momentarily light-headed. She splayed her hand over her chest, breathing deeply to regulate the rhythm.

Malik looked alarmed. "What is wrong? Do you need a doctor?"

She shook her head. "No, I'm fine. Just a few skips. Happens sometimes, usually when I'm tired. It's nothing."

Before she had time to do more than squeak a protest, he swept her off her feet and into his arms, cradling her against his chest as he turned and barked orders to the men surrounding them.

"Malik, for God's sake, put me down! I'm not hurt," she cried.

He didn't listen. She considered kicking her legs and fighting, showing him just how strong she was, but decided that bringing them both to the ground with a struggle was counterproductive.

"Please put me down," she begged as he began to move. "This is embarrassing."

People were staring at them, pointing, whispering. Malik seemed not to care. It was stunning to be held against him after so much time. Like plunging into a swimming pool with all your clothes on. He was hard, strong, and the heat of his body reminded her of another kind of heat they'd once shared.

He glanced down at her, his handsome features stark against the dark red background of the headdress framing his face. No one would ever mistake this man for anything other than a prince, she thought wildly. He was so sure of himself, so full of life and heat and passion.

She'd missed that.

No.

No, she was *not* going there. She didn't miss Malik. She didn't miss a single thing about him.

"We are not going far," he said. "I will put you down as soon as we are somewhere quiet, so you may rest."

She turned her head away as his long strides ate up the distance. The entourage hurried along with them, in front of them, their passage through the airport like the ripple of a giant wave. Soon, they were passing between sliding glass doors and into a quiet suite with plush chairs, tables and a bar at one end. Soft music played to the empty room. The lights in here were low, the air cool against her heated skin.

Malik set her down in one of the chairs. A glass of cold fizzy water appeared before she'd even blinked.

"Drink," he ordered, settling into the chair beside her and picking up the glass.

"I've had plenty to drink," she said, pushing his hand away. "Anything else, and I'll explode."

He looked doubtful. "Jahfar is hot, *habibti*. It can sneak up on you before you realize it."

"Water is not my problem, Malik," she insisted. "I've just flown all the way from L.A. I'm tired. I'm stressed. I want a bed and six hours of uninterrupted sleep."

She'd slept a little on the plane, but not enough. She'd been too nervous.

And with good reason. The man staring back at her now, this hard, hawklike being who seemed so remote and unapproachable—so regal—could make a lion nervous. Were they really married? Had she ever shared a tender moment with this intimidating man?

"Then you shall have it," he said. He nodded to a man who turned and disappeared through another door. A few minutes later, he took her hand—as she tried desperately to block the prickling heat of skin on skin—and led her out the same door and into an elevator. Then they were exiting the airport through a private entrance and climbing into a Mercedes limousine.

It was almost like the past, only Malik was dressed in white robes and a headdress instead of a tuxedo. He looked so cool and exotic while she felt frumpy and hot. She tugged at her jacket, drawing it off and laying it on the seat beside her.

Malik's eyes dropped to her chest, lingered. She felt his gaze as a caress, felt her body responding, her nipples tightening inside her bra. Lightning sizzled in her core. She crossed her arms and turned to look out the window.

"Where are we going?" she asked as the limo slid into traffic. In front of them, a police car with whirling lights blazed a trail. The windows were tinted dark, but the light outside them was still so bright. It would be blinding, she realized, were she out in it. And hot, as he'd said.

"I have a home in Port Jahfar. It is only a few minutes away, on the coast. You will like it."

Sydney leaned her head against the window. It was odd to be here, and exciting in a way she hadn't anticipated. In the distance, stark sandstone mountains rose against the backdrop of the brilliant sky. Date palms dotted the landscape as they rode into the sprawling city. The buildings were a mix of modern concrete, glass and sandstone.

She realized that the hills in the opposite direction weren't actually hills, but sand dunes. Undulating red sand dunes. Along their base, a camel train trod single file toward the city. It was the most singularly foreign moment she'd ever experienced.

The car soon left the stark landscape behind as they passed deeper into the city. Eventually they turned— and suddenly the sea was there, on her right. They rode a short distance along the coast, with the turquoise water sparkling like diamonds in the sun, and then they were turning into a gated complex.

Malik helped her from the car and ushered her inside a courtyard cooled with tiny jets spraying mist that evaporated before it hit her skin. The air was thick, hot. It wasn't unexpected, or even anything she'd never experienced before—and yet it was different in its own way.

Or maybe she was just too tired.

A woman in a cotton *abaya* appeared, bowing and speaking to Malik in Arabic. And then he was turning to her as the woman melted back into the shadows from whence she'd come.

"Hala says that your room is prepared, *habibti*. You may sleep as long as you wish."

She'd expected that a servant would show her the way, but Malik took her elbow—no matter how lightly he touched her, she still burned—and guided her into a huge sunken living area and down a hallway that led to a small suite. The outer room had cushions arrayed around a central table, a rosewood desk in one corner and two low-slung couches that faced each other across a fluffy white goat-hair rug. The bedroom featured a tall bed covered in crisp white cotton linens that beckoned seductively.

"I need my bags," she said, realizing suddenly that she had nothing to change into. They'd left the airport without collecting her luggage.

"They are on the way. In the meantime, you will find all you need in the bathing room." He gestured to another door. Sydney walked into the spacious bath, marveling at the sunken tub, a shaft of sunlight coming from high up in the ceiling and illuminating the marble. The light picked out the red and gold veins of the stone, sparkled in the glass mosaic tiles surrounding the tub.

"I trust it meets with your approval."

Sydney whirled, his voice startling her, though it shouldn't have. She'd known he was behind her, watching her from the door.

"It's lovely," she said, swallowing hard. Why did it feel so surreal to be here like this? She'd agreed to come, known it was necessary, and yet she felt off balance, out of her element in a way she hadn't expected.

And why not? This is Jahfar, not Paris, she told herself. *Not Los Angeles.*

Malik crossed to her, cupped her face in his hands
while her heart thundered in her ears.

She meant to protest, she really did, but her voice
froze in her throat.

"There is nothing to fear, Sydney," he said. "We will
get through this."

When he lowered his head, her eyelids fluttered
closed automatically. Because she was tired, of course.
No other reason.

He chuckled softly, his lips brushing her forehead
while her pulse throbbed. The sound speared into her
heart, reminded her of a different time when she still believed in a fairy tale ending with the handsome prince.

"Don't," she choked out as his lips moved to her
temple.

An instant later, he released her and took a step backward. "Of course," he said, his voice thicker than it had
been only a moment ago. "As you wish."

Sydney put a shaking hand to her throat, dropping it
again when she realized how frightened and helpless it
made her seem. She was neither of those things, though
she was most definitely nervous. She'd loved him. She'd
been through hell because of him. This situation was
strange, unnatural.

For them both, she thought. He would probably prefer to be with his current mistress instead of her, the
wife he'd thought he was rid of.

"I think it's best if we don't…touch," she said.

He arched an elegant brow. "You are afraid of a little
touch, Sydney? And here I thought I was resistible."

He was mocking her. Naturally. She lifted her head.
"There is no purpose to our touching, Malik. We aren't

happily married. We are nothing to each other. Not anymore. I realize I'm an inconvenience to you, but I just
want to get this over with. You don't have to pretend
otherwise to make me feel more comfortable."

His dark eyes flashed with emotion. "I see. How wise
you have grown, Sydney. How very jaded."

"I always thought you liked jaded women," she re-
torted—and felt instantly contrite. If she were trying to
make him believe they could behave with cool civility
for forty days, she'd just failed abominably.

He leaned against the door frame, but she didn't
make the mistake of thinking him relaxed. No, he was
carefully—and tightly—controlled. It had been one of
the things that had driven her the most insane about
him, that ability to shut down his emotions and rein
them in so hard that he was nearly inhuman.

"I did not realize you cared," he said softly. Mock-
ingly, still.

Sydney flicked her hand as if brushing away a fly.
"I don't."

He straightened to his full height. "Let us not de-
scend into games, *habibti.* You have had a long night
of travel. Bathe, rest. I will see you when you are prepared to be reasonable."

Her temper spiked at the condescension in his tone.
"I'm not playing games, Malik. I came, didn't I? I'm
here because I want this over with. Because I want to
be free of you forever." She flung the last at him, unable to stop herself from saying the words.

His jaw hardened, his eyes flashing hot once more.
"You will get your wish," he growled. "But first I will
get mine."

Her stomach flipped. "Wh-what do you mean?"

He looked so menacing. "Scared, Sydney? Afraid of what I will exact from you now that you are here?"

She swallowed, her throat thick with emotion. "Of course not."

His gaze slid down her body, back up, his eyes hot on hers. His voice came out as a sensual drawl that made heat flare in her core. "Then perhaps you should be."

CHAPTER FOUR

MALIK was in a bad mood. He sat in his study, working on minute details that were mind-numbing and boring and meant to distract him. They did not.

He shoved back from the computer and turned his head until he could see the sparkle of the sea beyond the windows.

She was here. His errant wife. The one woman he'd thought might be different, might make him happy—but who, instead, had run away from him. He was not accustomed to women running away from him.

It had been a singular moment when he'd realized she'd truly gone.

He'd raged. He'd made plans. He'd sworn to go after her and drag her back by force if necessary.

And then he'd thought, *no*.

She'd walked out. Let her be the one to come back. Instead, she'd started divorce proceedings.

Yet he still wanted her. His body desired hers, regardless of his wishing otherwise. From the moment she'd opened the door to the house in Malibu, he'd wanted her with a fierceness that surprised him after so much time.

Especially considering how very angry he still was with her.

But she'd looked so virginal, so pure, in her white jacket and pale pink dress. Her long legs had been displayed to perfection, enhanced by the nude-colored high heels she'd worn. He'd imagined those legs wrapped around him as he thrust into her body.

It had taken every ounce of control he'd possessed not to press her. Because he'd known that she still wanted him every bit as much as he wanted her.

Her body wanted him, but her heart did not. And that was what had stopped him, both then and today.

He squeezed the pen he held until it cracked, its jagged edge slicing into his finger. A drop of blood welled on the tip. He grabbed a tissue from the box sitting on his desk and swiped the blood away.

Sydney Reed—Sydney Al Dhakir, he corrected—was so beautiful, so very luscious, so bad for his control. From the first minute he'd seen her, he'd wanted her. She'd been aloof…but only at first. When he'd finally gotten her into his arms, she'd burned so hot he'd known that once with her wasn't enough.

She probably wasn't the most beautiful woman he'd ever known, but he couldn't actually remember another being more compelling to him. Her skin was as pale as milk, her hair the color of the red dunes of the Jahfaran desert. Her eyes were like a rain-gray sky, the kind of sky one often found hanging over Paris in winter.

While others might find rain depressing, he found it unbearably lovely.

Especially when it was reflected in her eyes.

Malik swore softly. He'd known, when he'd impulsively married her, that it could not last. Because he'd married her for all the wrong reasons, not least the utter dismay it would cause his family. That, and he'd wanted her with a fierceness that had shocked him.

The phone clanged into the stillness, making him jump. Though he could let his secretary get it, he preferred the distraction to his chaotic thoughts.

"Yes?" he barked into the receiver.

"I hear that your wife arrived today," his brother Adan said.

"That's correct," Malik replied somewhat stiffly. "She is here."

He'd kept her away from Jahfar for a reason. Now that she was here, he had no choice but to share her with his family. Though he'd thought there might be a bit more time before that happened. Malik frowned. His brothers would be polite, but his mother certainly would not.

"And do you plan on bringing her to the palace?"

Malik ground his teeth. He hadn't told Adan why Sydney was here. He hadn't told anyone. "Perhaps in a few days. Or not. I have business in Al Na'ir."

"Surely you can spare an evening. I wish to meet her, Malik."

"Is that a command?"

There was no pause whatsoever. "It is."

How very easily Adan had slipped into power. He hadn't been the heir to the throne, just as Malik had not been a part of the ruling family, until their cousin had died in a boating accident and Adan suddenly found himself the heir to their uncle. When their uncle died a year later, Adan had ascended the throne as king.

He'd been a good king. A just king.

"Then I will bring her. Though not today. She is tired from the journey."

"Of course," Adan replied. "We will see you for dinner tomorrow night. Isabella looks forward to it."

"Tomorrow night then."

Their goodbyes were stiff, formal, but Malik had expected nothing different. They'd had such a barren childhood, with nannies and a kind of rigid formality that was not conducive to warmth between them. Oh, Malik loved his brothers—and his sister—but theirs was not an easy relationship.

He wasn't quite sure why. There'd been no huge trauma, no major falling out. Just a quiet distance that seemed impossible to breech. The more time moved on, the wider the chasm.

Perhaps that was why he'd been so drawn to Sydney. She'd made him feel less alone, and he'd been addicted to that feeling. But that was before she'd betrayed him, before she'd proven she was no different than anyone else in his life.

Malik checked his watch. It had been over six hours since he'd brought her here. He debated calling Hala to check on her, but decided he would do so instead. He would not hide from her, would not shrink from the raw emotions still rolling between them like a storm-tossed sea.

He found her on the small terrace off her room, her long hair loose and flowing down her back, the wind from the sea ruffling the auburn strands. She'd put on a fluid cream-colored dress that skimmed her form. It was slightly darker than the milk of her skin, but it made her look ethereal. Like an angel.

She turned her head as he approached, setting down the coffee she'd been cupping in both hands. Her expression went carefully blank, but not before he saw the yearning there.

It gutted him, that yearning.

"Are you feeling refreshed?" he asked.

"I am, thank you," she replied, glancing away again.

He pulled out the chair opposite her, setting it at an angle so he could view the sea and her face at once if he so chose. "Your luggage is intact, I take it?"

"Yes. Everything arrived."

She picked up the coffee again, her long fingers shaking as she threaded them on either side of the cup. He did that to her, he realized. Made her as skittish as a newborn foal.

It reminded him of the first time they'd made love. She hadn't been a virgin, but she hadn't been terribly experienced, either. Everything he did to her had been a revelation. Soon, she'd been bold and eager for more.

His body hardened instantly.

This was the problem, he thought, with no small measure of anger. This need that flared every time he was with her. He'd ceased trying to understand it long ago. He'd never been the sort of man to be ruled by his penis—until Sydney came along and turned everything upside down.

He blew out a disgusted breath and turned to stare at the container ship gliding into port in the distance. It wasn't simply the physical that drew him to her.

No, he'd been dissolute long before Sydney came along. He'd indulged every appetite, every whim. It had been great fun.

At first.

But in the last couple of years, the more he'd pushed the envelope, the emptier he'd felt.

And she seemed to fill that emptiness somehow.

"I'm going to need internet access," she said, cutting through his thoughts. "I have work to do while I'm here."

"There is Wi-Fi," he told her. "I will have someone give you the password."

"Thank you." Her fingers drummed against the side of the cup. He heard her draw breath, as if she was planning to speak, but she said nothing. Several more times she tried, until he finally speared her with a look, pinning her into place.

"Say it, *habibti*."

She was looking at him with those big grey eyes, her long lashes sweeping to her cheeks and back up again as she let her doubts war with her desire to speak.

Then she bit her lip, and he forced himself not to turn away. Forced himself to deal with the slice of pain that shafted into him, the flood of desire that pooled low in his groin.

He would conquer this ridiculous need.

She was a woman, like any other. She was not special, or different. She possessed nothing that he couldn't obtain elsewhere. Whatever pull she had on him, whatever imagined void she seemed to fill…she was not irreplaceable. No woman was. He knew that better than most.

Her expression changed by degrees, turned fierce, and he knew she'd made up her mind. He relished her fierceness. It was far better than wide-eyed defeat.

"I want to know why you never brought me here," she burst out, gesturing at him, her hand encompassing his entire body as she swept it up and down. "This is who you are—the clothes, the desert—but you never let me see it."

She leaned toward him then, her eyes stormy. "Did I embarrass you *that* much?"

There, she'd said it. She'd finally put voice to the pain that had been nagging her since the moment she'd arrived and seen him dressed in traditional clothing. This was who he was. This was his life, his heritage, and he'd never allowed her to be a part of it.

She *knew* why, but she wanted to hear him say it. She wanted him to admit to her that he'd regretted taking her for his wife. Her heart thundered, her pulse throbbed and her breath razored in and out of her chest. She *needed* to hear him say it.

To her face this time.

Not that she was in any danger of forgetting, of succumbing to his considerable charm, but she wanted the pain front and center so long as she was here. If she kept it there, it would act as a shield.

He'd removed the headdress between the time she'd seen him earlier and now. His dark hair was wavy, thick, and she remembered threading her hands into it, pulling his mouth down to hers as she lay beneath him in their bed.

Her heart turned over at the thought. Warmth gathered in her belly. A knot of something she dared not name tightened in her core.

No. Those memories had nothing to do with now.

"You did not embarrass me." Malik's handsome face was carefully blank, and though the words were what she wanted to hear, she did not believe them. He was too stoic, too detached. "We would have come here eventually."

"Eventually," she repeated, unable to keep the bitterness from her voice. He would not tell her the truth, even now. Had she truly expected it?

"What do you wish me to say, Sydney?" he demanded. "It was not foremost on my mind, I have to admit. I was more concerned with how long I had to wait until the next time I could get you naked."

Sydney set the coffee cup down, grateful that she

didn't clang it into the saucer. "Why can't you just admit the truth?"

His dark eyes flashed, his expression hardening. "Why don't you tell me what this truth is and stop beating around the bush, as you Americans say?"

"You know what it is. You just won't say it."

He got to his feet, gazed down at her with that cool disdain she'd come to hate. He'd always shut down whenever she'd pressed him about anything. And she'd been so blinded by love that she hadn't seen it for the warning sign it was.

"If this is how you plan to spend the next forty days, we will never be divorced," he said.

She lifted her chin. She'd never really confronted him about anything. They hadn't been together long enough to truly argue, and she wasn't a confrontational person. But she was feeling so frustrated, so disoriented being here with him now, and she was fed up. Fed up with hiding behind a mask, with worrying that she didn't fit in or that she was embarrassing to those she cared about. She'd been trying to fit in since she was a child, and she was suddenly unwilling to do it with him for even a moment longer.

"Why is it suddenly my fault? Why am I the one causing the problem? You're the one who can't admit to the truth."

"I don't do drama, Sydney," he growled. "Either say what you so desperately want to say, or be quiet."

Fury roiled in her belly like a living thing. She pushed her chair back and stood, unwilling to allow him to stare down at her. Or to stare down at her from so great a height, she amended, since he was still taller than she was.

Fine, he wanted to hear it, she was not holding back

a moment longer. She'd already held back for far too long. Time hadn't eased the pain, but it had at least allowed her to come to terms with it.

"I think you *were* ashamed of me," she accused him. "And I think you didn't want to bring me here because you regretted marrying me."

His laugh was bitter. "And this is why you left me? Why you walked out in the middle of the night? Because of your own insecurities?"

"I left a note," she said, and felt suddenly ridiculous. A note? She'd packed her suitcase and fled because she'd been hurt, confused and suddenly so unsure of herself. She'd needed time to think, time to process everything. She'd never thought, never believed for a moment, that an entire year would pass without any communication from him. She'd been impulsive, reckless.

But she'd had to go. What choice was there?

"A note that said nothing. Less than nothing."

"Then why didn't you call me and ask for more?"

He took a step closer, his arms rigid at his sides. "Why would I do so, Sydney? *You* left me. You left. You chose to flee. You did not do me the courtesy of speaking to me first."

Sydney was trembling, but not from fear. A hard knot formed in her gut, her throat. The words wouldn't stay inside her. The bitterness she'd held in for a year came spilling out. "I heard you, Malik. I heard you tell your brother that you regretted marrying me. You were on speakerphone, in your office—"

The words died, simply died. She couldn't continue. His face said it all.

"*This* is why you ran away like a child? Because of

something you heard me say in a private conversation that you had no right to listen to?"

She swallowed. Her throat felt as if it were lined with razor blades. How dare he try to make her feel guilty! "You can't turn this around, Malik. You can't make it about me listening in on your private call when you plainly said you'd made a mistake. I wasn't trying to listen. I came to remind you that we were due at the opera at seven."

He looked so cold, so remote in that moment. She felt as if she'd violated his privacy when in fact *she* was the one who had every right to be upset. Damn it, he'd said he'd made a mistake! She'd been so desperately in love with him that she'd given up everything to go with him. Like some giddy schoolgirl with her first crush, she'd left her friends, her job and her home and followed him halfway around the world.

Because he'd asked her to. Because she'd believed he was the right man.

And then, when he'd suggested they marry, she'd been the happiest woman in the world. A little niggling voice had whispered doubts, but she'd ignored them. She'd been blind, thrilled, happy—and it had all come crashing down, just as she'd known deep inside that it must.

Girls like her didn't get the fairy tale prince, not really. She was pretty, she supposed, but she wasn't elegant. She wasn't sophisticated enough for a man like Malik. She'd ridden the wave as far as it would take her, and then she'd had to go before it crushed her.

"You did not leave that night," he said. "I remember the opera. It was *Aida*. You did not go for another week at least."

"Because I kept hoping it was a mistake! I kept waiting—"

His gaze sharpened when she didn't finish the sentence. "Waiting for what?"

She couldn't answer. Because she'd been waiting for him to say he loved her. A foolish hope in light of everything that happened.

They'd gone to the opera that night, her heart feeling as if it were being ripped in two, and then they'd returned home. He'd had business to attend to, he'd said, and she'd gone to bed alone. She'd lain awake, waiting for him, but he never came. She'd finally fallen asleep as the sun was creeping into the sky, her heart still breaking.

She'd learned in the week that followed that a heart did not break cleanly or quickly. It happened slowly, agonizingly, by degrees.

And it wasn't a sharp feeling, but a dull throbbing one that refused to go away. It was the kind of pain that permeated your entire body, your soul, and left you wanting to fall asleep and not wake up until it was in the distant past and you didn't feel anymore.

Malik grew cold, detached. He spent his days closeted in his office, or traveling on business. He became darker, quieter, harder to read. But at night, he would slip into their bed and take her again and again, the pleasure so hot and intense that it took her breath away.

Soon, she'd started to think she'd misunderstood his conversation. And one night, when she was boneless and spent, her heart throbbing with conflicting emotions that were killing her inside, she'd let spill the words she'd been feeling for weeks but hadn't been brave enough to say yet. She'd told him she loved him.

Sydney closed her eyes. Even now, the memory hurt.

He'd said nothing. It was as if he hadn't heard her, but she knew he had because his grip on her tightened for the briefest of moments.

She didn't know what she'd expected, though she'd had a vague hope he would tell her he loved her, too. When he said nothing, her last hope was crushed.

"Nothing. It's nothing."

His hand shot out, his finger tipping her chin up so he could gaze into her eyes. He was angry, yes, but he was also brimming with some other emotion she couldn't quite pin down. Her skin sizzled beneath his touch. Would there be a mark when he pulled his hand away? Would she be forever branded with the imprint of his finger?

"Do not lie to me. Not now." His voice was hard, dark, full of leashed fury.

"What does it matter, Malik?" she asked tiredly. "We're finished. It's over. What happened a year ago isn't important. It won't change anything now."

"Tell me, Sydney," he demanded.

She almost said it. Almost spilled her deepest desire to him. Her most foolish and misguided wish.

But he would pity her if she did. Right now, she still had her dignity. If she tore away that last veil, admitted her plaintive hope, she would reveal the depth of her foolishness to him.

Sydney jerked away, took a step backward as she crossed her arms over her chest. "You don't have the right to ask. And I'm not answering. It's *over*."

He stared at her, his jaw grinding—and then he swore. Explosively.

She took another step backward, both appalled and fascinated. She'd never, ever seen Malik lose his cool. Not once in the short time she'd known him. He was

a passionate man, but a supremely regulated one. His
rigid control never shattered.

"It's not over," he growled moments later, his accent
thicker than she'd ever heard it. "Because you are here,
Sydney, in Jahfar. You are my wife for forty days. And
I *will* have satisfaction."

She had no idea what that meant, but she shivered
as he turned and swept away from her in a magnificent
swirl of white robes. The air crackled in his wake, and
she found herself sitting in her chair, staring after him,
not quite remembering when she'd sat down.

Her stomach was hollow, her nerves stretched taught,
almost to the breaking point. Coming here had been a
mistake. Such a huge, huge mistake. She should have
tried harder to find another way.

But what other choice had there been? It was the law.

And she *had* to get through it. They both did.

But she was beginning to doubt that either of them
would make it through unscathed.

CHAPTER FIVE

SHE did not see Malik for the rest of the day, nor did she see him the next morning. In some respects, it reminded her of their days in Paris, after the first couple of heady weeks when they'd been inseparable. Except this time it didn't hurt so badly. She knew what to expect now, knew he did not love her.

Nor did she love him.

Malik was a prince, but he was also a businessman. He was lord of his own territory within Jahfar—Al Na'ir, she believed it was called—and he worked hard to make it profitable and self-sustaining. There was oil throughout Jahfar, but Al Na'ir had the richest wells. She remembered that he'd been working on a deal to modernize Al Na'ir's oil industry when they were in Paris.

Sydney logged on to her computer and did some work on new listings that were coming up. In the past couple of years, she'd somehow become the office's web guru. In truth, she loved playing with the site's design. It wasn't quite the same as painting pictures, but she hadn't done that in years anyway. A twinge of wistfulness crawled through her, but she pushed it away and concentrated on the website.

This at least was something of which her father could

approve. Something useful and practical, unlike art. She'd even thought of taking some classes in graphic design, of working to create things for people. It wasn't the same as painting, but it was artistic—and you could make money doing it.

She made a few last changes, and then uploaded the new page to the website. The blazing purple graphic she'd created for The Reed Team stood out, her parents' smiling faces gazing at her so confidently.

Now theirs was an admirable marriage. John and Beth Reed had met in college and been inseparable since. They'd married within a year, had two children, started their business and built it into something they could be proud of. Alicia, her older sister, was an over-achiever like their parents. She was blond, stunning and wildly popular when they were still in school. As an adult, she hadn't stopped excelling: a Rhodes scholar, Alicia had graduated at the top of her law class. She was a huge asset to The Reed Team now that they'd branched into commercial real estate.

Sydney slapped the laptop closed with more force than necessary. The old sibling rivalry was alive and well. She loved Alicia and applauded her success. But she'd always felt like the odd duck in her family of swans. She was the only fair-skinned redhead, the only artistic type, the only one who didn't get a visceral charge out of making business deals. When she was little, she'd thought she was adopted—but now she knew it wasn't true. She had her mother's bone structure, her father's eyes. She was a Reed all right.

But she was still the odd duck.

Lunch arrived sometime after the noon hour, served by Hala and a man who stood mutely by with the tray of food as Hala retrieved dishes and arranged them on the low table in the living area of Sydney's suite.

There were dishes of olives, hummus, baba gha-noush, and grilled lamb with tomatoes that was served over fragrant basmati rice. Hala bowed and backed away, the man with her following suit. When they were a certain distance from her, they pivoted and hurried out the door.

Sydney blinked, and then shook her head slowly. The only time Alicia had been the tiniest bit envious of her was when she'd started to date Malik. If her sister could see this, she would no doubt turn pea-green.

Except that appearances were certainly deceptive. There was nothing to be jealous of, unless Alicia had a burning desire to live with a man who turned her inside out—and not in a good way—for the next forty days. Since Alicia's current boyfriend basically worshipped the ground she walked on, Sydney doubted she'd want to trade places. Who would?

Sydney frowned. She had to stop comparing her life to Alicia's perfect one. It did no good and only made her feel worse.

"They do you honor because you are a princess," Malik said, and Sydney whirled to find him entering her rooms from the terrace. Today he was wearing a pair of khaki trousers and a crisp white shirt. Not so exotic as the *dishdasha*, but still unbearably handsome. Even in Western dress, he somehow managed to look as if he'd just ridden in from the desert on the back of a fiery Arabian steed.

Sydney's heart kicked up several notches as he met her gaze, her skin heating by degrees until she knew she must have been red in the face.

She couldn't help it. She was flustered, embarrassed and angry. Not a good combination.

"I wish they wouldn't," she said. "It makes me uncomfortable."

His sensual mouth flattened. "I know this. Why do you think I did not bring you to Jahfar before?"

Sydney tilted her chin up. "If that was your reason, why couldn't you have told me? Seems awfully convenient to say that now, Malik."

He strode toward her. She stood her ground until the last second, until he was nearly upon her. Just as she turned to flee, he sank onto the cushions arrayed around the table. She stared down at him, her heart still fluttering like mad. What had she thought he was going to do? Grab her and toss her over his shoulder? Take her to his bedroom and have his wicked way with her?

A tiny part of her whispered, *yes, please.* She ignored it as she moved to the other side of the table. Malik grabbed a piece of flat bread and dipped it into the lamb-and-tomato dish. Then he speared her with a look.

"Think what you wish, Sydney. You seem determined to do so anyway."

She stood there, undecided what to do next. She didn't like the fact that what he'd said made sense. Had he really considered her feelings last year? Had he tried to spare her the intense scrutiny that went with being his wife here in Jahfar?

Was it possible? Or was he just very good at making her feel petty?

She watched him eat, watched the slide of his throat as he swallowed. For a moment, she considered leaving. But where would she go? And why? It would simply make her seem even pettier than she already did.

Besides, the smell of the food was driving her insane.

It'd been a while since breakfast, and her stomach was about to eat itself. She sank onto the cushions opposite him. "I don't recall asking you to join me for lunch," she said, reaching for a dish.

"In fact, you are joining *me*," Malik replied, lounging sideways on an elbow. "I instructed Hala to set lunch in here."

Sydney looked away and popped an olive into her mouth. It was too intimate, eating with him like this. They'd shared meals before—some of them in bed—but this time was different. Harder because of the emotion she felt being here now. Knowing she'd given him everything, believed in him, and he'd only ever given her a very superficial part of him.

"Why?" she said. "I could have come to the dining room—or wherever you usually eat. Or I could have eaten alone. That would have been fine, too."

"Yes, but tonight we dine with my brother and his wife. I had thought we could use this opportunity for instruction."

Sydney coughed as the next olive lodged in her throat. "Your brother—the king?" she managed to ask when she'd swallowed it. "And his queen?"

"The king and queen of Jahfar, yes. They wish to meet you."

Heat prickled her skin again. She was so completely unprepared for everything this life entailed. No matter that it was temporary. Dinner with a king?

A king who had not been pleased with Malik for marrying her. "Is that a good idea? I'm not really here to stay."

He shrugged. "Probably not, no. But we are commanded to attend. My brother is curious, I imagine."

"Curious?"

"About the woman who enticed me to give up my cherished bachelorhood. Though she now wishes to divorce me."

Sydney cast her gaze down. The lamb she'd taken a bite of had been delicious—now it was more like a lump of sod in her mouth. "Please don't," she said.

"Don't what? Speak the truth?"

"You make it sound as if you are hurt. But you aren't, Malik. Your pride perhaps, but not you. Not your heart."

She could see out of the corner of her eye that he'd gone still. "How well you know me," he said, his voice containing that hint of mockery she hated. "I'm amazed at your insight."

Sydney closed her eyes and sighed deeply. "I don't want to do this right now," she said. "Can't we just eat?"

"We can," he finally said, reaching for another piece of bread. He tore it in half, handed one side to her. His fingers brushed hers as she accepted it, a tingle of fire rippling up her arm in response.

Why couldn't there have been another way? Why did she need to be here in Jahfar, living in Malik's house, eating with him, gazing at his once beloved face across a table and knowing their relationship was in its death throes? And now, as if it weren't painful enough, she would have to face the brother who knew that Malik regretted marrying her in the first place.

Beyond humiliating.

Sydney dipped the bread in the sauce the way he did, scooped meat and rice up together. She made the mistake of glancing at him after she'd put the food into her mouth. He was watching her intently, his dark eyes smoldering as they held hers.

Her stomach flipped. "What?" she said when she'd

managed to swallow. "Do I have sauce all over my chin?"

"Not at all." He took another bite of the food while she focused on the variety of dishes instead of him. "I was thinking that you seemed to appreciate your first taste of Jahfaran cuisine."

She was confused, nervous, and angry with herself for being so. Confused because he watched her so intently and she didn't know why. Nervous because she imagined he was cataloguing her flaws. And angry because she cared.

"It's good," she said. "I'm enjoying it very much."

Or as much as possible when the man who'd turned her world upside down sat across from her as if nothing bad or hurtful had ever happened between them.

"I am glad," he replied. "But tonight I imagine the fare will be more familiar to you. The queen is half-American and will no doubt wish to make you feel comfortable."

"That's really not necessary," Sydney said. "I like trying new things."

His gaze sharpened, and she knew with a certainty he wasn't thinking of food. "Yes, I remember this."

Sydney glanced away, her face reddening. The bad thing about being so pale was that there could never be any doubt when she was embarrassed. Everyone knew.

"You will need to wear an *abaya* tonight," Malik said while Sydney sent up a silent thank you that he did not pursue that line of the conversation. "I have ordered several for you to choose from. If we had more time, I would have them custom made. But the seamstress will be able to tailor one to fit for tonight."

"There's no need to have anything custom made,"

she said. "It would be a waste of money. And I will pay for the necessary garments myself."

"You are so determined not to accept anything from me. You were not always this way, I recall."

Sydney tugged at the napkin on her lap. It was true that she'd never protested when he'd spent money on her before. It hadn't seemed necessary then. She'd never asked him for gifts, but she'd never turned them down, either. "I see no sense in it. I don't want to feel like I owe you for anything."

"How odd," he said, his jaw tightening as he stared at her.

"Why is that odd?"

"Does this prohibition against owing me only extend to financial matters? Because I feel as if you still owe me something for the way you left like a thief in the night."

It was a direct hit, and yet it made her angry instead of remorseful.

"What could I possibly owe you for that?" she flashed. "You could have called me. You could have come after me. You did nothing. Because you knew you'd made a mistake, Malik. Because you wanted to be free of me but you didn't know how to do it!"

It hurt to say it, but it was true. He'd made a mistake, and she'd done the dirty work for him by leaving before he could push her away.

He looked so coolly furious in that moment. "Do you honestly believe I lack the necessary courage it would take to extricate myself from a marriage I no longer wanted?"

It didn't seem like him, and yet what else could she think? If he'd cared, he wouldn't have waited a year to come after her. Which he'd only done because she'd initiated divorce proceedings.

"I don't know what to believe." It was nothing more than the truth.

"The correct answer, Sydney, is no."

She pushed back on two hands and glared at him. "Then why did you say you'd made a mistake? Are you trying to tell me I didn't hear you correctly? Because I'm fairly positive I did."

A muscle in his cheek flexed. His eyes burned into her. "No, you did not hear incorrectly."

In spite of the fact she knew it to be true, a sharp pain pierced her heart to hear him finally say it. As if she didn't already know. As if she were hearing the words again for the first time. Ridiculous to feel so much when she'd had a year to think about what he'd said to his brother. And how he'd reacted when she'd confessed her love.

Malik stood. "I said the words, Sydney, though I did not intend for you to hear them. It was never my intention to hurt you."

Her head tilted back as she gazed up at him. Tears pressed at the corners of her eyes, but she'd be damned if she let one fall while he stood there. She would be strong, unfeeling.

Just like him.

"Then I'm not sure what we have left to talk about. You said you'd made a mistake. And now we're divorcing. Everything has worked out perfectly for you."

"Yes," he said softly. "Perhaps it has."

He glanced at his watch. He looked so cool, so controlled, while she felt like a mess inside. Her stomach fluttered, her chest ached and she was no longer hungry.

"The clothing will be here in an hour. Choose what

you like. Pay me if you wish. I care not." He inclined his head. "Until tonight."

Sydney had an overwhelming urge to throw something at his retreating back. Instead, she punched one of the pillows lining the seating area. It didn't help.

Malik felt nothing. She felt everything. And this was only day two.

CHAPTER SIX

SYDNEY dressed with care in the turquoise silk *abaya* she'd chosen from the selection the seamstress brought. She did not wear a headscarf, but she did twist her hair into a loose knot and secured it with a couple of rhinestone pins. She wore her own shoes with the outfit, a pair of kitten-heeled strappy sandals that didn't give her the height she would have liked but were very comfortable and modest.

She kept her makeup subtle, concentrating on her eyes and adding a touch of pink gloss to her lips. When she was satisfied she looked presentable, she grabbed her small clutch and went to meet Malik.

He was standing in the entryway, waiting. She hesitated when she caught sight of him, but he looked up just then and she could do nothing except stride boldly forward. He'd always been gorgeous in a tuxedo, but tonight he made her heart ache with longing. He wore a black *dishdasha*, embroidered at the sleeves and hem in gold thread. His *keffiyeh* was the traditional dark red. Somehow the framing around his face succeeded in drawing her attention to his mouth.

That bold, sensual mouth that had taken her to heaven and back.

She looked away, determined not to think about

it. And yet she could feel the heat rising, flaring beneath her skin. Between her thighs. A tingle of sensation began deep inside, whether she wanted it to or not.

How could she still be attracted to him when he'd hurt her so badly? He didn't want her, not really. He'd thought she was a mistake. It was too much like growing up in the perfect Reed family, where she was the imperfect one. The mistake. Her family was blond, tanned, gorgeous, ambitious, successful. She was none of those things.

"Do not fear, Sydney," Malik said, mistaking her inability to look him in the eye for shyness. "You look lovely. The king and queen will not find fault with you."

"Thank you," she replied. Because there was nothing else to say. Not without sounding pitifully insecure and needy.

Soon, they were exiting the house and climbing into a sleek silver Bugatti. The engine roared like a tiger as Malik accelerated onto the thoroughfare. She turned her head, gazed at the city lights instead of at him. The sports car was super expensive, but the interior was small. He sat so close to her. Too close.

She could smell his skin, the scent of his shampoo. She could feel his heat as if he were curled around her.

Or maybe that was her heat as her body reacted to him.

His voice sliced into the silence. "My brother does not know why you are here."

Sydney whipped her head around to stare at him. For a moment she wondered if she'd heard him correctly. But no, that was what he'd said. "You didn't tell him about the divorce? Why not?"

Malik's fingers on the wheel were strong, sure. She

dragged her gaze from them and concentrated on the stubborn set of his handsome jaw.

"Because it is our business, not anyone else's."

She could only gape at him. "But we've been apart for over a year. Don't you imagine he's suspicious?"

"People do attempt to reconcile, Sydney." He glanced into the rearview mirror, changed lanes smoothly and quickly. "Unless you wish to spill our personal problems tonight, I suggest you pretend to be happy."

Pretend to be happy. As if a river of hurt had not passed between them. As if she could simply flip a switch and act as if her heart hadn't broken because of this man. "I'm not sure I can do that."

He shot her an exasperated look. "It's not difficult. Smile. Laugh. Don't glare at me."

She folded her arms across her breasts. "Easier said than done," she muttered.

Malik's fingers flexed on the wheel, his tension evident. "It's one night, Sydney. I think you can handle it."

Ten minutes later, they were driving through the palace gates and pulling up to the massive entry. Malik told her to wait, then came around and helped her from the car. He tucked her arm into his and led her toward the entry. All along the red carpet lining the walkway, men in uniform bowed as they passed.

And then they were inside the palace, and Sydney was trying very hard not to crane her neck. She'd seen opulence before, of course. She'd shown houses to the very rich, and she'd lived with Malik for a month in Paris. She knew what wealth could do.

But this place was more than she'd expected. Crystal chandeliers, mosaic tiles, Syrian wood inlaid with mother-of-pearl, Moorish arches and domes, delicate paintings on silk, marble floors.

Her heels clicked across the tiles, the sound echoing back down to her from the vaulted ceiling. "Did you grow up here?" she asked, and then wished she hadn't spoken. Her voice sounded very loud in the silent rooms, as if she'd shouted the question rather than whispered it.

"No," he said curtly. His body was tense, but a moment later she sensed a softening in him. As if he were trying to follow his own advice and pretend they were not on the edge of disaster. "My family was not in the direct line for the throne. Adan came to power when our cousin died, and then our uncle afterward. It has been an adjustment for all of us, but for him most of all."

"'Uneasy lies the head that wears a crown'," she quoted.

"*Henry the Fourth, Part Two*," Malik said without pause.

"I didn't know you liked Shakespeare." They'd gone to the opera a couple of times, to the ballet once—but never to a play. Why had they never discussed Shakespeare? She'd wanted to study literature and art in college, but her parents wouldn't hear of it. It was a business degree or no degree.

Liberal arts majors worked in the food service industry, according to her father. Business majors made the world go around.

"There's a lot you don't know about me, *habibti*."

But before she could ask him anything else, they reached a door with two guards stationed on either side. One of the guards opened the door, and then they were entering what looked to be a private area that was infinitely homier than the palace they'd passed through.

A very attractive, but otherwise normal-looking couple came to greet them. It took Sydney a few moments to realize this was the king and queen of Jahfar. The pregnant queen, with her long tawny hair streaked with sun-kissed highlights, looked more like a California girl than Sydney did.

"Call me Isabella," the queen said when Malik introduced them. Sydney instantly liked Isabella. King Adan, on the other hand, was imposing. He and Malik were the same height and breadth, but Adan looked harder, harsher, more serious. The weight of that crown, no doubt.

And possibly the weight of his disapproval of her. Sydney dropped her gaze as he studied her. He was no doubt remembering that phone call. Hearing Malik tell him again that he'd made a mistake when he'd wed an American girl with no money or connections.

"Welcome to Jahfar, sister," the king said, kissing her on both cheeks. "You are long overdue for a visit."

"I—thank you, Your Majesty." She could feel the color rising, creating twin spots of flame in her cheeks.

Malik took her hand, pulled her to his side and anchored an arm around her. She was grateful for it, if only for the way it diverted Adan from studying her so intently. His gaze swept over them both, and then he was turning and leading the way to the dining room.

He was so like Malik. Intense, dark, handsome. They were clearly brothers, both with the same bronzed skin, chiseled bone structure and rich voices. And yet there seemed to be a coolness between them, a reserve.

Sydney thought she must be wrong at first, but all throughout the dinner she noticed how formal they were with one another. Like business associates rather than family.

It was Isabella who was the social butterfly, who smoothed the conversation when it reached a rough patch, who kept them talking when it seemed there was nothing else to say. She was warm and witty and full of personality.

For the first time, Sydney didn't feel so intimidated by what she thought life as a sheikh's wife must entail. Isabella was nothing like Sydney had expected—and that was a good thing.

When dinner was over, Isabella suggested they take coffee on the terrace—but not before she asked Sydney to accompany her to the nursery to check on her son.

"The truth is that I wanted to talk to you alone," Isabella said as she closed the nursery door behind them after their visit.

"Oh," Sydney said. "All right." She was still feeling entranced by Rafiq's dark curls, with the way he'd been lying on his back, his head to one side and his little leg kicked up. She'd not actually thought much about children with Malik, though she'd expected they would have had them after they'd been married for a while.

Now the thought made her heart squeeze tight.

Isabella took her hand and led her to a sitting area tucked away in an alcove. "I know it's probably difficult for you," Isabella said once they'd sat down facing each other. "It's not easy to put a marriage back together after so much time away. But I want you to know it's possible. Al Dhakir men are worth the trouble, even when you think you'd cheerfully strangle them and leave them for dead."

Sydney made herself smile. "Did the king give you trouble?"

Isabella laughed. "Far more than you'd like to hear about, though I think I was probably the one who caused the most trouble. But we survived it. And you can, too. Give Malik a chance. He's a good man—they all are—

but they don't always know how to reach out to the ones they love."

Love. Now that was definitely not an issue with Malik since he did not love her. But Sydney wasn't about to say so, especially when she could see how much the king absolutely adored his wife. His eyes smoldered when he looked at her. His expression lit up. He touched her often, even if it was just a light touch of his hand on hers.

Once, she would have given anything for Malik to feel that way about her. It was too late now, but she wouldn't say so to the queen.

"I'll remember that," she said, dropping her eyes from the earnest look in Isabella's. The queen truly believed what she said, and while Sydney was glad it had worked out for them, she knew it was hopeless for her and Malik. You couldn't put back together what had never been there in the first place.

Isabella squeezed her hand. "Good. Now why don't we go have that coffee, hmm?"

Thunder woke her in the middle of the night. Sydney sat up in alarm, her heart pounding, certain she hadn't heard correctly. This was a desert country—they didn't have thunderstorms. Or did they?

Another crash sounded, and then a flash of lightning. Sydney grabbed her robe and stumbled from the bed. A hot gust of wind rippled her clothing as she opened the doors and stepped onto the terrace in her bare feet. The stones were still warm from the afternoon sun. Another flash of lightning lit the sky, illuminating the sea and the thunderclouds hanging over the water.

It had taken her hours to fall asleep. Jet lag was partly to blame. Malik was the other part of the equation.

They'd driven back to his home in silence after dinner with the king and queen. Sydney had wanted to ask him questions about the evening, about his family, but she'd been unable to find her voice.

She'd kept expecting him to speak to her, but beyond a cursory question about how she'd enjoyed the food, he'd said nothing else. When they'd arrived, he'd bid her a good night and left her standing alone in the entry.

Another gust of wind blew her hair across her face. She shoved it to the side and breathed deeply of the rain-scented air. It reminded her of storms back home when she was a kid, of the way she'd made up stories in her head about giant knights slaying fire-breathing dragons in the sky.

Her father had said she was too fanciful. Alicia had always laughed and gone back to playing office with her dolls.

"It looks worse than it is."

Sydney spun to find Malik sitting at the other end of the terrace. He unfolded his frame from a chair, stalked toward her. Her heart was already hammering from the thunder, but it kicked up several notches as another flash of lightning illuminated the sky.

Dear God, Malik wasn't wearing a shirt.

Sydney swallowed as he came to halt in front of her. "Will it actually rain?"

He tilted his head up, exposing his throat as he gazed at the sky. She remembered nibbling that throat. Sucking the skin there. A dart of sensation throbbed between her legs. She could feel herself growing wet, feel the aching heaviness of sexual arousal. His chest was broad, sculpted with muscle. Lightly sprinkled with hair that tapered into a *V*, leading the eye down, down, down to the waistband of the faded jeans he wore.

Sydney jerked her gaze back up, but not quite in time. Malik was watching her, his dark gaze smoldering with intensity.

"Like what you see?"

She tossed her hair over her shoulder again. Why lie? He'd see right through her anyway. "Yes. But it doesn't matter if I like it or not, because I'm not traveling that road again."

His chuckle was a sexy vibration in his throat. "It won't rain here tonight, but we could quench our thirsts in other ways. I'm sure you remember how good it was between us, Sydney."

"I don't care," she said, her voice catching at the end.

He reached out with one hand, tucked a strand of hair that had blown free behind her ear. A shiver ran the length of her. He was different now. Not as reserved as earlier. After they'd left the palace, he'd been silent, tense. She'd wanted to know why, but she'd been unable to ask.

"You used to care. Very much. I remember that you couldn't get enough of me."

"People change, Malik. I've changed."

"Have you?"

"I think we both have."

"Perhaps these changes will only make it better," he said, his voice too seductive for comfort.

She *was* mesmerized. Oh, how she *wanted*. But it was a bad, bad idea. Once she stumbled down that path, she wouldn't be able to turn around again. Because he was addictive.

"I doubt that," she said firmly, as much to him as to herself.

His smirk told her she'd made a mistake. "Yes, perhaps you are right. It could hardly get better. How many ways did you give yourself to me? How many times?"

"More than enough," she answered, proud of herself for being able to reply when his words called up a wealth of erotic memories in her mind.

"I'm certain we could think of a few more things to try," he said.

She shook her head. "It won't work, Malik. You can't talk me into going to bed with you."

"Who said anything about a bed?"

A crash of thunder reverberated off the water and Sydney jumped. Malik caught her as she stumbled into him. He held her close, his heart thundering as fast as her own. His big body was so solid, so comforting. She felt like an ice cube dropped into warm water. She was thawing, melting, losing herself.

It had always been so with him. He had only to touch her, and she responded.

He shifted—and she felt the press of his erection against her body. Without conscious thought, she leaned into him. Malik sucked in a breath.

"Careful, *houri*," he growled in her ear. "Or you will find yourself in my bed before you know it."

She wanted to be there. Ached to be there. One more night with Malik, one more night feeling more alive than she'd ever felt in her life, more cherished…

No. He did not cherish her. He never had.

"I'm sorry," she said, pushing away from him. He let her go without protest, his arms dropping to his sides.

Her skin sizzled from the contact with him, her pulse throbbing—in her temples, between her legs.

"I'm sure it would be fabulous, but I'd still regret it in the morning," she told him. "It won't change anything between us. And it would make the remaining time together even more difficult."

"So we cannot be, how do you say, friends with benefits?"

A twinge of sadness curled through her. "We've never been friends. I think we skipped that part altogether."

Malik shoved a hand through his dark hair as he blew out a frustrated breath. "No, perhaps not."

Sydney bit the inside of her lip. That was not an admission she'd expected from him. "I feel like I know nothing about you."

"You know the most important things."

"How can you say that? I know nothing! Until tonight, I didn't even know you liked Shakespeare."

"I went to university in England. Shakespeare was inevitable."

"See, I didn't even know that much."

He spread his arms wide in frustration. "Then what do you wish to know? Ask me, and if I can, I will tell you."

Another peal of thunder sounded over the ocean. It was less violent now, less surprising. What did she want to know about Malik? Everything, and nothing. Everything because she knew nothing, and nothing because she didn't want to open herself back up to the pain of caring for him in any way.

But curiosity won out over restraint. "I'd like to know why you and your brother are so uncomfortable together."

He closed his eyes briefly. Pinned her with a hot glare. "Of course you would ask this. And I have no answer for you. We were close as children, but drifted apart later. Our lives were…formal."

"Formal?"

"You lived in a house with your parents, yes?" When she nodded, he continued, "We had nannies, and we did not always live in the same house. Our mother was… nervous, let us say. Children were too much for her."

"Too much?" A knot was forming in the pit of her stomach as she imagined the Al Dhakir children growing up without their mother.

She could see tension in the set of his shoulders, the thrust of his jaw.

"We saw her, but we were to be on our best behavior when we did. She preferred socializing with her friends to children. I think it was not quite her fault, really. She was young when she and my father married, and the babies came right away. She didn't know what to do with us, so she retreated behind the veil of wealth and privilege she was afforded."

"And your father?"

He looked sad. "A good man. Very busy. And very formal. I think he had little time for my mother, and so she had little time for us."

Sydney thought of her own parents, of how much they loved one another and how happy her childhood had been. Yes, she felt like the cuckoo in the nest, but she'd always been loved. Even when her parents were slightly alarmed by her tendencies, or disappointed in her inability to be more like Alicia, they loved her.

"But he must have loved her if he married her."

Malik's laugh was unexpected. "This is how marriage is supposed to work in *your* culture, *habibti*. Here, one marries for duty. For family alliances. To consolidate power and land. My father married the woman who had been arranged for him. And then he did his duty and got her with child."

Sydney felt sad. It was all so cold, so unfeeling. And yet it was the Jahfaran way. Who was to say America was any better? People married all the time for love— and love did not always last. You only had to look at the national divorce statistics to realize that.

And she was about to become another one. Odd in a way.

"You have not asked the most obvious question," Malik said, cutting through her thoughts.

She was still trying to process the idea of marrying someone she did not love in order to ally her family with another. "What is that?"

His gaze glittered. "You have not asked if I had an intended bride," he said, his soft voice in contrast with the sharp edge in his gaze.

Sydney's stomach flipped. An arranged marriage for Malik? She'd never thought of it. And yet...

"Did you?" she managed to ask.

His smile was bittersweet. "Of course I did. I am a Jahfaran prince."

CHAPTER SEVEN

SHE was looking at him with a wealth of hurt in her rain-grey eyes. Malik cursed inwardly. He'd never intended to cause her pain, and yet he'd failed miserably on that score.

Too many times to count.

"You had a fiancée?" she said.

He shrugged casually, though he felt anything but casual. "Dimah was not my fiancée in the sense that you think of a fiancée."

She shook her head, her long red hair rippling like silk in the night. The wind wasn't gusting so badly now and she was no longer shoving hair from her face. The silk of her robe clung to her frame, the breeze contouring the fabric around the peaks of her lush breasts.

His body was painfully hard. Had been since she'd walked onto the terrace, the wind blowing her robe open and exposing her legs. Legs he'd had wrapped around him a lifetime ago.

Legs he wanted wrapped around him again. Now. Tonight.

It had been too long. Far too long.

"I don't know what that's supposed to mean," she said, oblivious to his torment. "You were supposed to marry someone. You married me instead. Why?"

Malik drew in a sharp breath as her words sliced through the fog of his thoughts. The hurt was still there, the horror. The guilt.

He hadn't talked about it with anyone, hadn't wanted to. It was over and Dimah was dead. Nothing he said or did would bring an innocent girl back.

Lightning flashed again, illuminating Sydney's face. She looked confused, worried. For him, he realized with a jolt. She was worried *for him*.

He did not deserve her sympathy.

"She died," he said, surprising himself with the words he'd never spoken to another.

Sydney grasped his hand, squeezed. He felt the jolt of sensation down to his toes. What was it about this woman that always, always got to him? He needed nothing, needed no one. Not even her.

But he wanted her. Wanted the way he felt when she was near, when she touched him with her soft hands, smiled at him. When Sydney looked at him, he didn't feel like he wasn't worthy of being loved.

"I'm so sorry," she said.

"It is not your fault. It happened a long time ago." He'd been barely twenty at the time. Young and foolish.

"And you did not marry anyone else."

"I did not have to, no." He hadn't wanted to marry Dimah. They'd known each other since they were children, and had always been intended for one another. But Malik hadn't wanted her. Dimah was like a wraith, following him at a distance, hanging on his every word, looking at him as if he were the only person in the world besides her.

As they'd gotten older, her behavior changed, but only slightly. She became subtler with her adoration, but it was still there. He'd felt as if she were suffocating him, though he rarely saw her and never spent time alone with her.

And then he'd thrown a fit when his father had summoned him and told him it was time for the wedding to take place. He'd been angry, and he'd gone to Dimah, railed against her.

"She killed herself," Malik said, remembering. "Because I told her I hated her."

He didn't miss the sharp intake of breath, the little gasp. She would despise him even more now.

"Oh, Malik." And then she squeezed his hand again. It was meant to be comforting, but the gesture was somehow more important to him than that. More profound. "It wasn't your fault."

He could still see Dimah's face. The way he'd crushed her dreams. "How could it not be? We were to be married, and I told her I hated her—because without her, I wouldn't be forced to do this thing."

"You aren't responsible for her actions," Sydney insisted. "No one is. She made a choice."

Malik could only stare. He wanted to believe, but he would not do so. Because he deserved to feel the pain of what he'd done. "She would not have made this choice if I'd quietly done my duty."

"You don't know that."

Her fingers were threaded through his now. He wondered if she knew it. He raised their clasped hands, turned hers over until he'd bared her pale wrist. Pressed his mouth there because he'd been dying to do so.

He felt the shudder pass through her. But it wasn't a shudder of revulsion.

"Why are you so willing to forgive me this terrible crime?" he asked. "You of all people should know how selfish I can be."

"I—" She dropped her gaze from his. He felt…disappointed somehow. Because now she would agree with him. There was no other choice. "Everyone is selfish from time to time. It doesn't mean you're at fault for what your fia— What Dimah did."

A surge of feeling blazed inside. She was wrong, of course, but he loved that she defended him. Was that why he'd gone against everything he'd known was right and married her?

He remembered meeting her, remembered the way her long legs had intrigued him as she'd walked in front of him and talked about the houses she was showing him. And then she would turn from time to time, quite surprisingly, and glare at him. As if she were daring him to say something, anything, that would give her the excuse she needed to end the appointment.

He'd been captivated, not only by her fierceness, but also by the way she dealt with him. As if he weren't the least bit attractive to her. He'd found that novel, considering the way women usually behaved when they discovered they were dealing with a bachelor prince.

Not that he didn't enjoy the fawning, the coyness, or even the downright bold ways in which women usually approached him.

But he'd never been treated with thinly veiled hostility. And it had intrigued him.

"How good you are to defend me," he murmured against the delicate skin of her wrist. "I remember that you did not always feel so charitable toward me."

Her head came up then, her eyes sharp and blazing with emotion. "I still don't. But I don't think you should blame yourself for another's actions, no matter how dramatic."

"Is it not my fault that you left me in the middle of

the night with hardly an explanation? Is it not my fault that you are here, now? I cannot be blameless in everything, *habibti*, though I appreciate that you would make me so."

"I—I made my own choices," she whispered harshly.

Lightning blinked in a chain of succession over the sea. It was like a series of lights being turned on for only a second before flashing out again. Thunder followed, but it was farther away and no longer seemed to frighten Sydney. She was watching him with eyes that were full of emotion. The air crackled with electricity, but he wasn't sure if it was the storm or the tension between them.

He wanted to pull her into his arms again, wanted to find out. He could lose himself for a few hours.

An impossible wish, however. She hated him. And he probably deserved it.

He let go of her hand, stroked along the skin of her throat with a finger. She swallowed convulsively, but made no move to stop him.

"Ah, but now you see the trap you have set for yourself, yes? In exonerating me of the crime of Dimah's death, you must also hold me blameless for your flight. For our estrangement. And that you cannot do."

Her eyes flashed. "Stop putting words in my mouth, Malik."

He would love to put something else there. He was not so bold as to say so.

"I only speak the truth."

She blew out a breath, tightened the belt of her robe. The outline of her breasts made his mouth water. "Neither of us is blameless," she said. "Neither is perfect." She rubbed a hand over her eyes. "I could have done things differently. I probably should have. I should have been more direct with you. Instead, I allowed you to control everything."

His head came up. "I was not aware of this. I remember you challenging me on more than one occasion."

She snorted. "For little things, Malik. Nothing big. Nothing important. And I should have."

"Yes, you should. I would have welcomed it."

Her laugh was soft, surprising. "Would you now? I hardly think so, oh, mighty prince of the desert."

"You mock me," he said, and yet he wasn't bothered by it. On the contrary, he found it amusing. Refreshing.

"No, I'm merely pointing out the truth."

He clasped her shoulders. His blood rushed from the simple contact. "The thing I liked about you from the beginning was your lack of pretense. You did not pretend to be overwhelmed by me."

She laughed. "God, no. I think I did everything but insult you to your face. I was a bit, um, hostile."

"Because you did your homework," he said, remembering what she'd told him once they'd started to see each other.

She looked down, clasped her hands together in front of her. "You didn't need yet another woman falling at your feet. Though it didn't take long for you to make me do just that, did it?"

Something sharp stabbed him in the chest. He remembered her surrender, remembered the sweetness of it. He'd never once believed it to be because she was weak. "I took your indifference as a challenge."

"Some challenge," she said bitterly. "It took you less than a week to succeed in making me forget my resolve."

"You are angry with yourself for this, yes?" Pain throbbed inside him. Filled him.

She regretted her capitulation. Regretted him.

A burning need to possess her, to make her forget every moment of hurt feelings between them, rose up inside him like a wave.

Why now? Why here? She did not want him any longer, as she'd been only too happy to tell him more than once since her arrival. He should have pursued her when she'd left Paris, should have refused to allow more than a day to go by where they did not speak about her reasons for leaving.

He'd been a fool.

"It would have been better for us both had I shown more restraint. We would not have to endure this time together now."

Her words stung. *Endure.* He did not like to think too deeply about that word, or the impact it'd had on his life thus far. There were many things in this life to be endured. It was not altogether pleasant to be one of them.

"And yet we shall." Sudden weariness washed over him. The evening had been a strain, in more ways than one, and Sydney was still looking at him with a kind of wariness that gutted him. He had no more patience for it. If he did not leave her now, he would scoop her up and take her to bed, prove that she could still be mastered by his touch.

And neither of them would gain anything by such a demonstration.

Malik took a step backward, bowed to her. "It is late, *habibti.* You need your rest."

Then he pivoted and strode away from her. Back to his bedroom. Back to his solitude.

Sydney did not sleep well. There were things she wanted to ask Malik, things she'd meant to say when they'd

stood on the terrace together. He'd been so approach-
able for once, so raw in his feelings. It was a side of him
she'd never seen before. She'd been drawn to him—a
dangerous feeling—and she'd wanted to know more.

But he'd shut down again. Withdrawn. Left her
standing there with the wind and lightning and her
tangled emotions.

She'd considered following him, but dismissed the
thought as foolhardy. He would be angry if she did so.
Not only that, but how could she control what might
happen if she followed him to his bedroom?

Because she was so weak where he was concerned.
She could still feel his chest where she'd pressed her
palms against him. The hard contours, the blazing heat
of his skin, the crisp hair. She'd ached with want. With
memories of bliss.

And when she finally did fall asleep, she was troubled by dreams of him, by the agony in his voice when
he'd told her about Dimah. Why had he never told her
before? Why, in the weeks they'd been together, had
he never told her?

It was another symptom of everything that had been
wrong between them. Everything she'd been too blind
to see. They'd barely known one another, subsisting instead on reckless passion and heated lovemaking. That
could only last so long before it burned itself out.

After a restless night, she awoke early. The sun
was just creeping into the sky when she showered and
dressed in a fitted mocha sheath and a pair of gladia-
tor sandals. Then she put her hair in a ponytail and applied the barest of lipstick and mascara before making
her way to the dining room.

Her heart thudded in her throat as she paused outside the door. She could hear Malik's smooth voice as

he spoke with one of the staff. Sydney sucked in a deep breath and walked into the room.

Two sets of eyes turned to look at her. Malik's dark gaze was angry, but it was the woman with him who drew Sydney's attention. She was slender, elegant, expensively dressed—and livid.

Definitely not a staff member.

She turned back to Malik, spewed a tirade of Arabic at him while gesturing to Sydney.

"Mother," Malik said at last, his voice harder than she'd ever heard it, "we will speak in English for the benefit of my wife."

His mother? Oh, God.

The other woman glared at her. "Yes, English. And you say this girl is not unsuitable to be an Al Dhakir? She does not even speak Arabic!"

"Language can be learned. As your command of English proves."

His mother bristled in outrage. "You should have done your duty, Malik. Your father let you off too easily after Dimah died. Adan found you a suitable bride, at my request, but you would not do what you should." The rings on the princess's fingers glittered in the morning light as she took a sip of her coffee.

"I preferred to find my own bride. Which, as you see, I have done." Malik looked murderously angry as he came over and snaked an arm around her. Sydney had no idea what his intent was—she was still stunned by the news that Adan had found Malik a bride, and that he'd refused to marry her.

When Malik pulled her close and dropped a kiss on her lips, Sydney could only gasp.

"Mother, you will greet my wife properly. Or you will leave."

"Malik," Sydney began, "that's not necessary."

His grip on her tightened. "It is completely necessary. This is our home."

His mother got to her feet in an elegant flurry of fabric and jewels. "I was leaving anyway."

Sydney watched Malik's mother start for the door. Her pulse was pounding. Her head throbbed. She felt suddenly hot, uncomfortable. This woman was Malik's mother—and she despised Sydney, not for any other reason than because she was a foreigner who had married her son.

No wonder he'd been reluctant to bring her to Jahfar. But she couldn't let him do this, couldn't allow there to be hard feelings between mother and son on her account. Not when there was no reason for it.

"Tell her the truth, Malik," Sydney said, stepping away from the circle of his arm. She had to play this cool. Collected. She could feel Malik's disapproval as she went and poured a cup of coffee for herself.

Malik's mother stopped and turned to her son. "Tell me what?"

Malik looked furious. And not with his mother this time. "Now is not the occasion," he growled.

"When would you suggest is a better time?" Sydney asked. "Tell her what she wants to hear. Don't torture her."

Malik's mother looked from her son to Sydney. She was a small woman, slim and graceful, with the same hawklike eyes as her sons. She looked fierce, proud. Also like her sons, Sydney thought.

"Malik?"

He didn't look at his mother. Instead, he was looking at her. Glaring at her. "Sydney and I are discussing a divorce."

It wasn't quite what she'd wanted him to say, but it was enough. It certainly had the desired effect, as his mother seemed to visibly melt with relief.

"Very sensible of you," she said. She turned to where Sydney stood with her coffee. "I'm happy to see that you do have some sense after all. You must know you don't belong here."

Sydney tilted her chin up. "I know it very well."

She'd once hoped against hope that it wasn't true, but she knew she didn't belong in Malik's life. She'd had a year to figure it out. And even if she hadn't, the last couple of days had driven the message home with sonorous finality. Sydney Reed was not meant to be a prince's wife.

Malik's mother nodded before sweeping from the room in a cloud of perfumed silk. Malik did not follow. He stood there, scowling. Sydney pulled out a seat and sank down into it.

She felt remarkably calm somehow. As if she'd faced the deadly storm and come out on the other side stronger for it. And yet, there was a slight tremor in her hand as she set her cup down.

"There is no need to glare at me, Malik. She was going to find out eventually."

"Yes, but when I wanted her to."

He was coldly furious, she realized. Her sense of having survived the storm began to ebb. "Why keep it a secret from everyone? It's not like we're trying to make this relationship work. We're coexisting for a purpose. I don't want to pretend this is something it isn't."

She didn't want any false hope, any magical thinking that would have her starting to believe there was something more between them. Her heart couldn't take it. A shiver slid across her skin, left goose bumps in its wake.

Because, yes, that was a problem. Being here with him, living with him, being inundated with memories—she was in danger of wanting too much, of believing there was a chance he could love her in return.

Love her in return?

Sydney shoved that thought away with all her might. She would not go there, would not dwell on the past and her feelings then. She did not love Malik. Not anymore. She couldn't.

How could she, when their conversations lately had proven she'd never really known him at all?

"Once you have finished your breakfast," Malik said softly—too softly, "you will need to pack your things."

The coffee cup arrested halfway to her mouth. Her heart dropped into her toes. "You're sending me away?"

He looked almost cruel. "That would not please you, would it?"

"Well, um, it would mess up the, uh, the divorce," she said lamely, her heart thudding a million miles a minute.

"Never fear, Sydney. You will get your precious divorce." The last word was hard, cold. Bitter. "But I have business that is long overdue in my sheikhdom. We are traveling to Al Na'ir without delay."

CHAPTER EIGHT

THEY traveled by helicopter. Malik piloted the craft with the expertise of someone who had done so many times before. Yet another thing she had not known about him, Sydney thought sourly. He sat in the pilot's seat of the military-like craft, his copilot beside him. They wore headsets and communicated from time to time, with each other and with what she presumed was a flight control tower somewhere.

Sydney sat in the back and gazed out the window at the scenery below. The landscape whisked by in the two hours it took to reach Al Na'ir, the red dunes and sandstone cliffs becoming more and more imposing as they flew. For once, she wished she'd bothered to look up Al Na'ir on the map. She knew nothing other than what Malik had once told her—that it was oil-rich and remote.

When the helicopter finally began its descent, she was stunned to see there was nothing around it. They landed on a rocky outcrop, the desert undulating in all directions. The land was barren, stark. There were no buildings, no house.

But there was a Land Rover, she noted with relief. A white vehicle sitting not too far from the landing area. The rotors slowed to a gentle *whop-whop-whop*. Malik descended, and then came to the rear of the helicopter and opened her door. A blast of hot air hit her in the face, taking her breath along with it.

What kind of barren hell was this?

"Where are we?" she managed to ask, grasping Malik's hand and letting him help her to the ground. She'd changed into a white cotton *abaya*, because he'd told her it would provide better protection from the elements, and a pair of ballet flats. The rocks beneath her feet were hot. The sun bore down on her head, its rays intense. It had not yet reached its zenith, but it was already scorching.

His dark eyes gave nothing away. "We are in Al Na'ir."

"But where in Al Na'ir?" she pressed. Because this was so remote she could almost believe they were the only people on the planet. It was a frightening feeling in some ways.

"We are in the Maktal Desert, *habibti*. It is the most remote area of Jahfar."

Sydney swallowed. "And why are we here? Is there more to Al Na'ir than this?"

"Much more. But we are here because I have business."

She eyed the Land Rover. "Where do we go from here?"

"There is an oasis about an hour's drive away. We will find shelter there."

Shelter. Sydney tried not to let her fear show. She'd never been anywhere so menacing before. "Why did we not simply fly there?" she asked as he reached into the helicopter and grabbed her suitcase.

The copilot came around and helped gather their luggage.

"Sandstorms are a problem. We cannot fly into the deepest desert because the sand will disrupt the engines. We would crash, Sydney. Here, we are on solid rock. It's as close as we can get to where we have to go."

"And is driving safe?"

"So long as the engine does not overheat, yes."

They carried the luggage to the Land Rover and stowed it. Malik said something to his copilot in Arabic. The man replied before bowing deeply. Then he was striding toward the helicopter and climbing inside.

"Get into the car, Sydney," Malik said. She did as he asked, buckling herself in as he slipped into the driver's seat. The rotors on the helicopter began to beat harder—and then the craft was lifting off and banking toward the horizon.

Sydney's heart felt as if it would beat out of her chest. The helicopter was gone, and she was completely alone with Malik in the middle of a harsh desert. If the engine died, would anyone find them?

"Why did he leave?" she asked.

Malik turned to her. "The helicopter cannot stay in the open. If there's a storm, the sand will gum up the engines. When we are ready to leave, it will return."

"And when will that be?"

"A few days, perhaps. No more than a fortnight."

A fortnight? She did the mental calculation—two weeks. Two weeks in the desert with Malik? She hoped it would not come to that. At least in Port Jahfar, she'd felt as if she could escape into the city if she needed time away. There was shopping, culture, activities.

But out here?

The journey to the oasis took longer than an hour. The sun was high overhead, but Malik did not have the air-conditioning cranked on high. It was warm in the Land Rover, though not oppressive.

"To keep the engine from overheating," he explained, though she did not ask.

They took a fairly flat path through the dunes, though occasionally they rolled up one impossibly high dune to slide down the other side. When she saw a stand of palm trees in the distance, she breathed a shaky sigh of relief.

They pulled to a stop beneath some trees as a group of black-clad men came toward the SUV. They were strong men, fierce men, with piercing dark eyes and sun-wizened features. And they were armed, Sydney noticed, with daggers and pistols clipped to their leather belts.

"Bedu," Malik said. "They will not harm you."

"I didn't think they would," she replied. Though they did look quite menacing.

Malik climbed from the car and spoke with the Bedu. The men bowed and made obeisance, and then a couple of younger boys were collecting the luggage and carrying it away. Malik came and helped her from the car, and then they were moving across the oasis and toward a large, black tent set beneath a stand of palms.

A shimmering pool of clear water gleamed in the sunlight in the center of the oasis. On one bank, a group of camels and horses stood contentedly, swishing flies with their tails. It was so odd to drive through a stark landscape, and then to come upon water in the middle of seemingly nowhere.

"Where does it come from?" she asked.

Malik followed her gaze. "From a reservoir in the sandstone deep below the surface. It has been there for millennia," he said. "At one time, this oasis was a vital stop on the trade routes between Jahfar and the north. It is what made the Maktal navigable."

Sydney imagined the oasis swirling with activity, camel trains coming and going as they followed the trade routes. There was a touch of romanticism to the idea, and yet she knew it would have been a hard life, a life filled with deprivation and danger. Much better to be here today. To arrive by air-conditioned car rather than on the back of a camel.

As she watched, three women trekked to the pool's edge and began to dip out water into a large trough. Sydney stopped when she realized they were washing clothes.

Malik came to a halt beside her. "It is their way," he said, as if he knew the sight surprised her.

"It's so surreal. What would they think if they knew about washing machines?"

Malik laughed. "They might be less impressed than you would imagine. This is a way of life that is very ancient."

So much for romanticism.

They continued walking toward the tent. The men who'd led the way were waiting at the entrance. Malik spoke to them, and then they were moving away, toward another group of tents at the other end of the oasis. Machinery began to hum nearby. It surprised her, though perhaps it should not have.

"Did they know you were coming?" she asked, shading her eyes to watch them go.

"I have not been here in quite some time. No, they did not know I would arrive today. But this is my land, and I am their sheikh, and therefore they are prepared for me."

He held the flap open for her and Sydney ducked

inside. The confines of the tent were hot, the air still. Malik strode past her and did something she couldn't see. Then a fan blasted on high. It didn't cool the air much, but it moved what was there.

"There is a generator," he explained. "It won't run an air-conditioning unit, but it will run fans and lights. And refrigeration," he added. "It has only just been switched on, but soon there will be cold beverages."

"Amazing," she replied. A generator in the desert? That explained the machinery she'd heard. "But why this oasis, Malik? What's here for you?"

Because she was baffled. If there were a large oil industry nearby, they would have power and workers and the infrastructure to support them. There would be no need for a tent in the middle of a desert that seemed about as far from anywhere as you could get.

He looked away, busied himself with turning on other fans. "I have neglected to visit the Bedu. It was time I came."

Sydney licked her lips. "It could not have waited?"

He turned, speared her with hot dark eyes. "No."

Sydney let her gaze wander over the tent. It was luxurious, she realized, with bright carpets on the floors and walls, hammered brass tables and even a low-slung couch. What she didn't see was a bed.

"Where do I sleep?" she asked.

"There is a bedroom."

She looked around, realized there was a shadowed opening that must lead to another section of the tent. And then what he'd said sunk in. "A bedroom? As in one?"

"Yes, one."

Her pulse kicked into high gear. One bed. "That

won't work," she said, hoping her voice didn't sound as husky as it felt.

"I cannot create another bedroom, *habibti*. This is what is."

"I'm not sleeping with you."

He sauntered toward her, finally halting only inches away. She could feel his heat enveloping her. Her gaze landed on his mouth. That gorgeous, sensual mouth. His lips were full, firm, oh, so kissable.

"Perhaps you should," he said, his voice a sexy purr. "Perhaps we should explore every nuance of this marriage before ending it permanently."

"You can't mean that." Her heart was pounding, her stomach flipping. Need was pooling in her blood, filling her veins, making her body throb. She could feel the wetness between her thighs, the ache of arousal.

"I might. After this morning's display, I'm beginning to think I've acquiesced far too easily to your demands."

Sydney blinked. "My demands? You're the one who forced me to come to Jahfar! I'm simply trying to get through this without a lot of pain for either one of us."

His eyes narrowed. "You have changed, Sydney. You did not used to be so…cynical."

She swallowed. "I'm not cynical. I'm just practical."

"Is that what they call it now?"

"You're still angry with me because of your mother," she said after a tense moment of silence in which she wasn't quite sure how to respond. "I'm sorry if you didn't agree, but I couldn't let there be hard feelings between you when there was no need for it."

His sudden laugh was harsh, startling. "I'm afraid you failed, my dear. There have always been hard feelings between my mother and I, and there will continue to be long after you are gone. Your outburst did nothing to relieve that."

She hurt for him, for the casual way in which he could say that he and his mother were at odds. But then she remembered what he'd said about his childhood, and all she felt was sadness. He'd been raised in wealth and privilege, but he'd never really known what it was like to have a close-knit family. His was all about duty and tradition—without any consideration for love and connection.

She thought of what his mother had said this morning about finding Malik another bride—and it felt as if a puzzle piece suddenly clicked into place. *Of course.*

"You married me because you didn't want to marry the bride they'd picked out, didn't you?"

"I married you because I wanted to."

"But doing so got you out of another arranged marriage."

He hesitated a fraction too long. "It doesn't matter."

"It does to me," she said, her heart throbbing with hurt. She'd been convenient, nothing more. If he'd been dating some other woman at the time, he would no doubt have married her instead. Anything to throw a wrench into his family's plans.

"Perhaps I married you because I felt something," he said, his voice dipping. "Did you ever consider that possibility?"

An ache of a different kind vibrated in her heart. "You're just saying that. Don't."

Because she couldn't take it, not now. Not when she'd spent the last year apart from him, not when he'd failed to contact her even once during their long separation. Those were not the actions of a man who felt anything.

Never mind the conversation she'd overheard with his brother. A conversation he did not deny having.

His eyes gleamed in the darkened tent. "You know me so well, don't you, Sydney? Always positive that you have my motives pegged. My emotions."

"You don't have any emotions," she flung at him. He stiffened as if she'd hit him, tension rolling from him in waves.

Her heart lurched, her throat constricting against a painful knot. She shouldn't have said that. This was a man who'd told her, with such anguish, that he'd been responsible for the death of a girl.

Malik felt things. She knew he did.

But she still doubted he'd ever felt much for her. Nevertheless, that did not give her the right.

She dropped her gaze from his, swallowed. There was no moisture in her mouth. "Forgive me," she said. "I didn't mean that."

He sounded stiff, formal. "I think we both know you did."

You don't have any emotions.

Malik couldn't put the words out of his head, no matter how he tried. The sun had sunk behind the dunes hours ago now, and the desert air chilled him. He sat with a group of Bedu who'd gathered around a fire, smoking *shishas* and drinking coffee. He let their talk wash over him, around him. He spoke when necessary, but always his mind was elsewhere.

You don't have any emotions.

He had emotions, but he'd learned at an early age to bury them deep. If you didn't react, no one could hurt you. He'd stopped crying for his mother when he was three, stopped crying for his nanny at six.

And he'd grown determined, the older he got, that
no one would force him to do what he did not want to
do. Ever. He'd had little choice when he was young, but
once he'd reached the age of majority, he'd been determined to make his own decisions, regardless of what
his family thought.

He was the third son. His recalcitrance would be an-
noying, but not shattering. Indeed, his father, beyond
the marriage with Dimah, had seemed in no rush to
arrange another wedding for him. But once Adan became their uncle's heir, his mother grew determined to
see each of her sons married and producing heirs. No
doubt to consolidate their family's grip on the throne.

As if it were necessary. There were at least four Al
Dhakirs who could inherit—and there would soon be
more since Isabella was pregnant.

He'd always intended to take a proper Jahfaran wife.
When he was ready. But first he'd wanted to have fun.

You have no emotions.

He could still see Sydney's face, the paleness of her
skin. She'd looked drawn, tired. Her voice had shook
as she'd accused him of marrying her to avoid another
arranged marriage.

He'd denied it, and yet—

She had not been entirely wrong. He'd known what
awaited him in Jahfar when he'd met her. He'd simply
been putting off the inevitable.

But then she'd become a part of his life, and he'd
wanted her in a way he'd wanted no one else. And, for
one brief moment, he'd thought, *why not?*

He'd known how she felt about him. And he'd never
once believed he was taking advantage of those feelings.
He was a wealthy prince, considered one of the most
eligible bachelors in the world, along with his brothers.

The woman he married would be fortunate. Honored. He was a great prize, a catch beyond compare.

Malik frowned. He'd been proud, arrogant, certain he was right. Certain he was making her life better when in fact he seemed to have made it worse.

She'd loved him once. He knew that she had, even if she'd only said the words on their last night together. She'd loved him.

But not enough. If she had, she wouldn't have run away.

His grip on the *shisha* tightened. There was nothing left between them now but passion. She might not love him, but she did want him. He would have to be made of stone not to know it. He could feel the electricity between them when she was near, feel the way she quivered with anticipation. When he touched her, she leaned into his touch. And she fought with herself until she won the battle and pushed him away.

His body ached with need for her. He remembered her touch, her scent, the feel of her beneath him. He missed that. He wanted to possess her again, wanted to own her mouth and her lush body. Wanted her to admit she wanted him, that maybe they had unfinished business left between them.

He'd brought her out here because he was angry. But also because he wanted to leave behind all the distractions of Port Jahfar. Out here in the desert, there was nothing but space and time.

Nothing to distract them. Nothing to interfere.

Malik climbed to his feet and thanked the Bedu for their hospitality. Then he stalked toward the tent where he'd left his wife.

* * *

Sydney lay in the big bed beneath a pile of furs. She'd been shocked at how cold the air grew after the sun went down. Malik had sent a Bedouin girl with food earlier, but she hadn't seen him since earlier in the day when he'd left her alone in the darkened tent with her heart in her throat.

Why could they not be in a room together without wounding each other? Why did every conversation between them degenerate into a battle of words, of old hurts flung so carelessly?

Sydney shoved a hand behind her head, stared up at the darkness. A small light burned nearby, throwing a purple glow into the room. She'd thought it was an oil lamp at first, had even managed to say the words in Arabic, but the Bedu girl smiled and shook her head as she flipped a small switch in the back.

A sound in the other room lodged her heart in her throat. She sat up, dragging the covers up with her. Waiting. What if it wasn't Malik? This was a wild, untamed place—even her cell phone didn't work, much to her dismay. What would she do?

A long shadow appeared on the wall, and then a man stepped into the room.

"Malik?" Her voice was little more than a whisper.

"You are awake," he said.

Relief made her sag into the mattress. "Yes. It's so quiet here." Not just that, but she'd been wondering about him. Worrying about him.

He began to remove his clothing. She could see the fabric whisper over his head, see the gleam of his bare chest in the lamplight. Her breath caught in her throat.

"I—I didn't know when you'd be back. I'll move to the couch in the other room."

He sat on the edge of the bed and pulled at his boots. "No," he said, and her heart skipped.

"No? I won't sleep with you, Malik, and I won't have sex with you," she said in a heated rush.

"So you keep saying. But I don't believe you, Sydney." He stood, still wearing the loose trousers he'd had on beneath the *dishdasha*. They hung low on his lean hips, tied at the waist with a drawstring. His hipbones protruded from the waistband, and her mouth went dry.

Oh, dear God. His abdomen was as tight as ever, his chest sculpted with lean muscle. His body was perfect.

Her heart throbbed. And, God help her, her body was responding.

"You won't force me," she blurted.

He put his hands on his hips. "No, I won't. But I won't have to, will I?"

Before she knew what he was planning, he grabbed her foot and dragged her down until she was lying flat on the bed. And then he was on top of her, his body hovering over hers but not quite touching.

His head dropped, his lips skimming her throat. She splayed her hands against his chest, intending to push him away—except that she didn't quite manage to do so. Heat seared her, glorious heat.

She arched her neck, bit her lip to stop the moan that threatened.

"You want me," he said, his voice a sensual rumble against her skin. "You burn for me."

"No," she replied. "No…"

"Then push, Sydney," he urged heatedly. "By God, push me away. Or I won't be responsible."

CHAPTER NINE

SYDNEY was frozen, like a small animal trying to hide from a much larger predator. She wanted to be strong, wanted to push him away—and she didn't. She wanted him with a fierceness that no longer surprised her. She wanted him inside her, his powerful body moving with precision, taking them both to heaven and back.

Her fingers curled, her eyes closing. Oh, how it hurt to want her desert prince so badly. To know that she would never truly have him, even if she offered herself up here and now.

She thought he would kiss her, thought that her inability to move would bring him to her and begin what she wanted oh so desperately.

Instead, he rolled away from her.

Sydney blinked back tears—of frustration, of anger, of sadness? She was no longer certain. Being with Malik again confused things. Confused her.

"Why did you leave, Sydney?" He sounded almost tormented. "We had *this*—and you left."

"You know why," she said, pushing the words past the ache in her throat.

"No, I don't. I know what you told me—that you overheard my conversation—but why did that make you go? Why didn't you confront me?"

"Confront you?" she choked out. "How could I do that? You humiliated me!"

"Which should have made you angry."

"It did make me angry!"

He rolled onto his side to face her. "Then explain to me how you thought leaving would fix the problem."

Sydney scrambled up to a sitting position. Shame flooded her. How could she say it? How could she explain that she'd always known she wasn't good enough for him? That she knew it was too good to be true? It had always been a matter of time before he no longer wanted her.

So why did you agree to marry him?

"I was upset," she said. "Hurt. You didn't want me, and I wasn't about to stay and pretend I didn't know it. And then, then…" She couldn't finish, couldn't speak about their last night together when she'd told him how she felt and been met with silence. It was too humiliating, even now.

"When did I say I didn't want you?"

She thought back. He'd never actually said those words, had he? But what else could he have meant when he said marrying her was a mistake?

She shook her head. He was trying to confuse her, and she wouldn't allow it. She had to hold onto her anger, her pain. "You told your brother you made a mistake. What was I supposed to think?"

He reached for her hand, took it in one of his. She tried to pull away, but he wouldn't let her. "I did make a mistake, Sydney. Because I married you without giving you a chance to realize what this kind of life entailed. Did you know my mother would despise you? That you would always be an outsider in Jahfar? Did you have any idea what being my wife would entail? I gave you no chance to discover these things."

Her heart hurt. Her head. Her throat felt like sand. "Are you really trying to tell me that you were only thinking of me when you said it? Because, if so, why didn't you come after me? Why didn't you call?"

"You left me, Sydney. No other woman has ever done so."

She couldn't believe what he was saying. And yet she could. Because Malik didn't love her. His pride had been hurt, but not his heart. He was not about to come after her when it was a matter of pride alone. She bit her lip to stop the trembling. Damn him!

She shook her head again. "It doesn't matter, though, does it? Even if we'd talked about it then, we're still wrong for each other. It would have never worked out." She swallowed. "A divorce is the right thing to do."

"Maybe it is," he agreed. "But the terms have changed."

Her heart fell to her toes. "I don't understand."

He sat up, faced her. His voice, when he spoke, was firm. "If you want this divorce, you're going to live with me as my wife."

She couldn't stop the gasp that caught in her throat. "That's not what we agreed to back in California!"

"This is the desert, *habibti*. Conditions change. We either adapt or die."

"But—but—this is blackmail," she bit out, fury vibrating through her. How dare he change the terms midcourse!

"I am aware," he said coolly. "But it is my price. If you don't agree, you are free to leave. We will simply remain married for all eternity."

Sydney struggled to calm her breathing. She was absolutely livid. And frightened.

"You would like that, I suppose." It would forever keep him from his family's matchmaking attempts, which he probably considered a good thing.

"Not particularly. It would require me to break our marriage vows since I refuse to spend the rest of my life celibate."

Sydney snorted. "As if you haven't done so already." She'd read the papers, seen the pictures of him with other women. She was not so naive as to believe he'd spent the last year completely alone.

"Ah, yes," he practically snarled. "Once more, you know me so well. You are quite an expert on my behavior. Whenever I am uncertain how to proceed, I should ask you in future. You will know unerringly what I should do."

"Stop it!" The words tumbled from her, laced with bitterness and pain. "Don't lie to me, Malik. Don't treat me like I'm stupid."

He swore, long and violently, in Arabic. "What about the way you treat me? As if I have no honor, as if my word means nothing."

"I didn't say that!" He turned things around on her, made her feel wrong for saying such a thing—and yet she'd seen the papers, seen the pictures of him with other women. How could the evidence be wrong?

"But you did." She could feel the anger vibrating from him, the indignation. A thread of doubt began to weave its way through her brain. "Do you know what I think, *habibti*? I think you are little more than a spoiled child. You refuse to deal with anything. You only wish to run away when life gets difficult."

A sharp pain lodged in her breastbone. "That's not true."

But she feared it was. She'd grown so accustomed to hiding behind masks, to hiding who she was and what she wanted. It had been the only way to survive, to be like everyone else.

To make her parents proud.

She was afraid to say what she wanted, afraid she would be rejected or ridiculed.

He reached out, his fingertips sliding along her cheekbone. "You have to grow up sometime, Sydney. You have to face your fears."

The lump in her throat was too big to swallow. "You're trying to change the conversation. It was about you, about your women—"

His hand dropped away again. The air between them grew frosty. "Yes, of course. Now please tell me how many women I've had. I seem to have forgotten."

His voice was tight with anger, but she refused to be intimidated. It felt wrong somehow to continue, and yet she blundered on. "There were pictures. You and Sofia de Santis, for one."

"Sofia is genuinely beautiful. She is also engaged— to a woman."

Sydney sucked in a breath, the fire of humiliation creeping up her neck. She was only glad it was dark and he couldn't see. How had she missed the news that Sofia de Santis was a lesbian?

"What about the Countess Forbach? There were several pictures of you together."

"No doubt because I attended many of her charity balls where I donated money to her causes. She is also, I must say, happily married to the count."

"You have an answer for everything," she said.

"And you have an objection."

"You can't really just expect me to believe everything I read was a lie—"

"Why not? Did any of these *news* articles appear in a real paper? Or were they splashed across the pages of the tabloids you grabbed at the checkout stand?"

"Why are you doing this?" she asked, anger and fear overwhelming her. Because he made sense and she didn't like it. Because if she believed what he said, she had to question everything about herself, about the way she'd run from Paris and hidden from the problem, convincing herself with each passing day that she had been right to go. "Why can't we just do what we were doing, endure this forty days and be done? Why do you have to make it into something more just to torment me?"

He grabbed one of the pillows from beside her and punched it. She flinched in the darkness, but he only tossed it down and stretched out, tucking it beneath his head. "What good has maintaining the status quo gotten us so far? We live as man and wife, or you return to L.A. without your precious divorce."

"That's not much of a choice," she whispered.

He yawned. "Nevertheless, it is the choice before you."

She sat there, aching, not knowing what else to say, how else to convince him. How would she ever survive being his wife again? How would her heart survive? He would destroy her. Once more, the wave that was Malik was dragging her under.

And there was nothing she could do about it.

"I'm going to sleep on the couch," she finally said, needing to say something, needing to contradict him, if only for the time being.

His only answer was a soft snore.

* * *

Sydney reluctantly trudged to the couch and fell asleep. She didn't want to leave the warm, soft bed—or the heat of the man beside her—but she felt as if she had to take a stand, no matter how temporary. But when she awoke the next morning, she was in the bed, snuggled beneath the covers—and Malik was gone.

It embarrassed her to think that he must have carried her there, and that she'd slept through the whole thing. How was that possible? But clearly it was.

She rose and went to wash in the bathing area, which was remarkably well-fitted for a desert tent, complete with a shower stall and solid surround, then dressed in a cool white *abaya* and sandals. The same girl from last night—Adara—brought her breakfast, which she ate in the living area while watching satellite television.

There was a news piece on a Hollywood couple, and she watched with interest as the familiar scenery of L.A. slid by. Remarkably, she didn't feel homesick for it, though she did wish for her own apartment—her own things. She wondered what her parents were doing. They'd been happy when she'd told them she was going to Jahfar with Malik. Having a prince for a son-in-law was quite good for business, it seemed. She hadn't the heart to tell them the truth.

She knew they would be disappointed in her when she returned alone, but the one thing about her family was they would never say so. In fact, they'd never said a word about her choices for as long as she could remember.

Unless it was a business decision, her parents said nothing. Her sister had always been her closest confidante—but Alicia had been tangled up with a new boyfriend for the past six months and was rarely available if she wasn't at work. Sydney had wanted to talk to her sister about what spending time with Malik again would mean, but Alicia could never take her calls.

Jeffrey needed her, or Jeffrey had other plans. Alicia would say a hurried goodbye, and the phone would go dead. Though they worked in the same building, lunches were also out because Alicia spent them with Jeffrey.

Sydney had a sudden feeling she should call Alicia, but her cell phone didn't work out here in this remote location. She would have to wait until Malik returned and ask him if there was a way to make a call. She assumed there had to be, since he had satellite television.

When she got bored of television, she ventured outside. The heat was staggering. She pulled the head covering tighter and walked toward the gleaming pool in the center of the oasis. The oasis seemed empty, but she knew it was not. The black tents of the Bedu were still erected on one end of the area, and occasionally she saw movement as a child darted outside and back in again.

Sydney skirted the far edge of the pool, intending to walk all the way around. It wasn't far, but at least it was a bit of exercise. A group of camels lay beneath the palms, tethered to a line, watching her progress while they chewed their cud.

At some point, she realized it was getting harder to breathe. She sucked in air that nearly scorched her lungs. Sweat trickled between her breasts. Her throat seemed to close against the heat, quickly devoid of all moisture. Finally, she stumbled to the foot of a palm and sank to the ground.

She put a hand over her stomach. It was beginning to ache, and her head felt fuzzy.

A few moments later a noise grabbed her attention and she looked up again. A horse and rider blotted out the sun. The horse was dark, brown or black, and finely made. Its nostrils flared wide, and red tassels dripped from its breastplate and bridle. One hoof pawed the ground impatiently. The rider, clad from head to toe in black, separated from the horse and sprang to the ground beside her.

"Sydney." The word was muffled behind the black fabric wrapped over his face. But the eyes…

"Hello, Malik," she said. "I was taking a walk."

Malik swore. And then he swept her into his arms and strode toward the tent. She expected he would set her down on the couch, get cool water for her, but he carried her through the tent and into the small bathing area. Once there, he turned on the water and pushed her under it fully clothed.

Sydney gasped as cold water rushed over her, soaking her to the bone. "What are you doing?"

He ripped away his face covering. "The heat is too dangerous. You should never have gone out in it."

"For heaven's sake, Malik, I was barely outside five minutes! I'm not dying!"

Though she might if he kept the cold water running on her like that—except that it sort of felt good sluicing over her. Perhaps she'd been hotter than she'd thought.

"You were overcome." One hand held her firmly under the water. His sleeve was soaked, but the rest of him remained dry as he refused to let her go.

"It was only a moment! I needed to sit."

"Where did you think you were going? This is the Maktal Desert! You could have been killed, if not by the heat, then by a scorpion or a viper."

A viper? Sydney shivered, and not from the water.

"I just wanted to go somewhere other than this tent! I was bored, and you weren't here…." She trailed off, realizing how ridiculous she sounded. Exactly like the child he'd accused her of being only last night.

"A very good reason to risk your life," he growled.

Sydney closed her eyes, fury and frustration welling within her. She had to do something or burst with it. Without thinking about the possible consequences, she cupped a hand and slung water at Malik. It hit him in the face, dripped down over his tanned features. One drop clung to his lower lip, and a dull ache began in her core.

No.

She would *not* want him. She lashed out again, slinging more water at him, soaking the front of his *dishdasha*.

"This is how you wish to play?" he asked dangerously. Then he shoved the dark covering from his hair, let it fall as he pushed her all the way under the spray, water rolling over her face for the first time.

Sydney came up sputtering. And furious.

She reached for him, wrapped her hands in the fabric of his clothes. She didn't expect she could move him, but she threw all her weight backward—and he stumbled into the shower. Water plastered his dark clothes to his body, and Sydney burst into a fit of giggles at the look of surprise on his face.

"How do you like it?" she asked.

His face was thunderous—but then he shoved his wet hair back and grinned at her. Her heart lurched. "I like it just fine," he said, his gaze dropping over her. Sydney glanced down—and squeaked in surprise. Her white garments were transparent. It wasn't quite like being naked, but close enough. The fabric clung to her, outlining her breasts, the dark nipples, the shadowed cleft between her legs.

She looked up again, met his hot gaze. The raw lust she saw there threatened to double her over with need.

Everything was happening so fast, the atmosphere between them changing, becoming more charged, more desperate.

"Malik," she choked out as he closed the distance between them. She wanted him—and she didn't. It terrified her to think of making love with him again—and it terrified her to think of *never* doing so.

She didn't know what he would do—but she realized his hand was shaking as he reached out. Shaking as he palmed her breast, his thumb brushing over the jutting peak of her nipple. Sensation streaked through her. Flames licked at her belly.

The water did nothing to cool this fire eating her up inside. Because nothing could cool her now. The fire needed to burn out, and the only way it would burn out...

"You've done it now, *habibti*," Malik said, smiling roguishly.

Her heart thrummed. "D-done what?"

He took her hand in his, pressed his lips to her upturned palm.

And then he placed her hand against his chest before sliding it oh, so slowly down his body.

CHAPTER TEN

THE wet fabric molded to his perfect frame, delineating muscle and sinew—but Sydney didn't need to see how the fabric clung to know he was hard.

The evidence—powerful, impressive, mouth-watering—thrust against her palm.

She couldn't take her eyes off his beautiful face. His eyes were bright, his jaw set in stone as if he were enduring a great torment. Sydney's body was aching, melting, throbbing with need. Touching him like this...

She swallowed. She knew that she had only to drop her hand away and he would turn and go.

Instead, she traced the hard ridge, her pulse thundering in her ears. He sucked in a breath, his eyes burning even brighter if that were possible. Then he pulled her to him, wet body to wet body, his arm hard around her. He hesitated only a moment before he dipped his head and covered her mouth with his.

There was never any doubt she would open to him. Her lips parted, her tongue tangling with his on a moan. He gripped her tight, kissed her with all the pent-up frustration and want that had been building between them.

His hands began to move on her body, divesting her of her clothes. She wanted to laugh—with joy, with nervous anticipation. This was Malik, her husband. The man she'd loved.

For one wild moment, she thought she should have said no, should have stopped him.

But it was too late now.

Too late.

She would play with fire and hope she survived.

As her clothes peeled away, the air from the fans cooled her even more. Goose bumps prickled across her skin. Malik broke the kiss to let his eyes travel her body. She dropped her gaze, self-conscious and unsure.

"You are beautiful," he said, his voice husky. And then he picked her up and sat her on the waist-high ledge surrounding the shower.

His dark head lowered. He took one tight nipple in his mouth, sucking it lightly while she squirmed and gasped. She could feel her sex tightening, swelling, aching with need for this man.

As if he knew it, he slipped a finger over her, caressed her silky curls, traced her outer lips. His finger glided into her moist heat, and she groaned with pleasure.

"Ah, Sydney," he said, "I've missed this."

Her heart squeezed even as pleasure rippled through her. *I've missed this.* Not, *I've missed you.*

But her thoughts fractured as he sunk a finger into her. A second joined the first, and then his thumb parted her, ghosted over her clitoris. She thought she would weep from the painful need he evoked. It had been so long, too long....

"Malik—"

"Yes," he murmured. "Yes. I have not forgotten even a moment of making love to you. I know what you need, *habibti.* I know what you want."

His mouth closed over her other stiff nipple, and she threw her head back as he sucked harder this time. A sharp current of pleasure spiked from her nipple to her clitoris, making her moan with need. He repeated the motion again and again, driving her insane for him.

She wanted him. Fiercely. Now. Deep within her, driving her—driving them both—toward completion.

But he would make her wait for it. She knew that.

Malik was the consummate lover. He was attuned to her body as if it were his own. He knew how to make her shudder and jolt and beg and cry. He knew how to wring every last bit of sensation from her, until she was utterly spent. Until all she could do was lay boneless and content and wait for her strength to return.

It had always been this way with him, this headlong rush into hedonism that was so unlike her. Nothing had ever made her want to abandon herself to pleasure. Nothing but Malik.

It frightened her, this dark need for him. She shouldn't be here, shouldn't be allowing herself to fall so hard again—but she was powerless to stop it from happening. She didn't *want* to stop it from happening. If she had to crash and burn, what a way to go...

His fingers moved in and out of her body, his thumb working against her sensitive bud until she knew she would fly apart at any moment.

But it was too soon. She didn't want to go over the edge yet. She'd waited so long now that she wanted to prolong the pleasure for a little longer. Prolong the torture.

"I want to see you," she cried. Somehow, she did not know how, she managed to form the words. Managed to speak them.

His dark eyes gleamed bright as he straightened. His fingers ceased their torture. "Then strip me, *zawjati*."

She looked at his traditional Jahfaran clothes, at the wet black material, and frowned. "I don't know how."

"I will help you."

She hopped off the ledge and he guided her hands to the fastenings. It took her only a moment to figure out how to rip them open. And then she was peeling the wet robes off, revealing his naked torso while he chuckled at her.

"So eager. I like this."

She couldn't stop herself from touching him, from running her hands over the peaks and valleys of muscle and sinew. The hard planes of his body that made her mouth water, made her long to press her lips just there and taste him again.

Malik might be wealthy and privileged, but he was a son of the desert. The kind of man whose strength wasn't feigned, but real strength forged from the harshness of the environment he came from.

Though he probably maintained his physique in a gym, he didn't look like the kind of man who jogged on sterile treadmills or lifted cold bars of steel. He looked as if he'd been formed during hot, hard work beneath a blistering sun.

Sydney frowned at the trousers and riding boots he wore. Those boots weren't coming off easily, and she didn't want to wait. She untied the trousers and slipped them open until they hung low on his hips.

And then, because she couldn't help herself, she pressed her hot, open mouth to his nipple as she found the hard ridge of his erection and squeezed. Malik sucked in a sharp breath, his hands coming up to cup her head.

"This won't last if you keep doing that," he warned her.

Sydney smiled against his skin. She loved knowing

she could make him dance on the edge of control. And when he lost that control…oh, God, it was spectacular.

The water was no longer flowing over them. She wasn't sure when he'd turned it off, but she was glad. Now, all she could taste was Malik. The warm honey of his skin. That combination of soap and man that she loved so much.

She trailed her tongue down the valley between his pectorals, skimmed over his tight abdomen. And then she freed him from his trousers and took him in her mouth while he made a sound that wasn't quite human.

His entire body stiffened. She glanced up. His head was tilted back, the muscles in his neck corded tight, as if he were fighting for control. His hands gripped the back of her head, fisted in her wet hair.

She swirled her tongue around the silky head of his erection. Her hand shaped him. He was like velvet and diamonds. So soft, and so hard at once. She wanted to bring him to completion this way, but he wasn't going to allow it.

He pushed her away, put his hands around her hips, and lifted her onto the ledge again. She clung to him, her mouth finding and fusing with his, their tongues tangling deeply and urgently.

And then she felt him, felt the hot head of his penis as he began to push inside her. She shifted her hips so she could take him deeper. She was impatient, needy. Greedy.

Malik held her hard, the tips of his fingers digging into her hips. She knew it was because he needed to hold onto his control, no other reason. He'd always been so rigidly controlled, even here—until he broke and let the passion overwhelm him.

She welcomed the fierceness of his passion. Craved it. Could not wait for the storm to break.

Sydney wrapped her arms around his neck, arched her body toward him. She wanted to drink him in, wanted all of him. *Now.*

But Malik was still in control. He pressed forward slowly, so slowly—and then he thrust to the heart of her, making them both groan with the exquisite pleasure of his possession.

He broke their kiss, pressed his lips to her jaw, her throat, while she clung to him. He didn't move, but she could feel the length of him throbbing deep within her. It was exquisite, this joining. She remembered why she'd been helpless before, why she'd followed him halfway around the world. Why she'd believed enough to marry him, though a part of her had known the truth.

She wasn't a weak woman, wasn't a particularly sensual one—except with Malik. Whatever he wanted, when they were like this, she would give.

Her hands slipped over his shoulders, down his back, trying to bring him closer as she arched and wiggled her hips toward him. His intake of breath was sharp.

"Sydney," he said, his voice broken. On the edge.

Exactly as she wanted him.

"Now, Malik," she urged. "Now."

He gripped her hips harder still—and then he withdrew, pulling so far out she thought he was planning to leave her insatiate and aching.

And then he thrust forward again, joining them once more. Sydney wanted to laugh with joy—and yet her breath froze, her lungs incapable of filling as the pleasure washed over her in blistering waves.

He thrust again, and then again—and her body caught fire until she was shuddering, until her very fingertips sizzled with the force of her orgasm. She was caught, too quickly, her entire being folding in on itself before bursting into a million liquid shards.

She knew she cried his name, knew that he was feeling a special kind of male triumph in that moment. He owned her, body and soul, and he knew it. She wanted to damn him for it, but she couldn't.

She wanted more—more Malik, more pleasure, more of his hard length thrusting into her.

She knew—without asking, without words—that he'd regained his strength. That somehow her surrender was required for him to be in control again.

Such exquisite control.

"Are you all right?" Malik asked.

Sydney shook her head, buried her face against his throat. His pulse throbbed in his neck, letting her know that he wasn't quite as controlled as she'd thought after all. The pieces of her slid together, reformed into something that she didn't quite recognize.

Or rather, something she *did* recognize, and dreaded. A woman who *needed*.

Malik tilted her chin back with a finger. His eyes searched hers, and the concern she saw there made her heart lurch. "Did I hurt you?" he asked, his voice so tender.

"No," she said. Then again, stronger, "No."

There were different kinds of hurts. But she knew he was talking about physical pain, and that was definitely not a problem. Emotional pain was another story.

"Good," he said. "Because I need you, Sydney. I need you."

And then he was kissing her again, and she was opening to him, taking him deep inside. He held her hips hard, thrusting into her, their bodies melding together. His strokes were deep, expert, driving.

She gave herself up to him, gave herself up to the rhythm and beauty of it. Sydney wrapped her legs around him, arched her body so that her breasts could press against his bare chest.

His mouth moved over her throat, his voice saying words in Arabic, and then he bent and took her nipple in his mouth, pulling hard so that the spike of pleasure shot to her sex. She was on fire for him, her body primed and ready for another shattering orgasm.

She felt as if she were swelling with something too wonderful to be contained, as if she would fly apart any second. Malik's thrusts grew more frenzied, his hold on her tighter.

And then his hand slid between them, finding her sweet spot, sending her over the edge.

She splintered apart in one long wave, coming with a gasp, his name spilling from her lips.

It did not end there. She was holding on to him, shuddering, her legs wrapped high around his hips as continued to pump into her. But his strokes were slower, more deliberate.

Not so frenzied.

And she knew he was drawing this out, giving her every moment of pleasure he could while waiting to take his own.

"Malik," she said. But it came out as a sob.

"Again, Sydney. I want to watch you come again."

She squeezed her eyes tight, tried not to focus on the sensations beginning to build in her core. Because she would be senseless in his arms if she let him keep taking her over the edge like this.

"I can't," she cried.

"You know you can." It was a firm command.

And then he lifted her up, his big hands splaying

across her bottom as he carried her out of the bathing room and into the bedroom. Their bodies were still joined. His gaze was hot on hers, intense. She wondered how he did it, how he kept such a tight rein on his need.

But she pushed the thought away because she didn't want to go there. Didn't want to consider that she might not mean anything to him, that he was capable of this because he had no emotional attachment.

Because it was just sex.

He put a knee on the bed, tumbled her back onto the mattress. And then he was withdrawing from her, sliding down her body. Before she could protest, he slid his thumbs into her sex, spread her open.

His tongue touched her hot flesh, his mouth closing over her clitoris. He suckled the sensitive flesh there with the same intensity as he'd shown to her nipples. His tongue darted over her, his teeth nibbling oh, so gently.

Her release sucked the air from her lungs. She sobbed his name, begged him to stop.

But not because it hurt, and not because she didn't like it.

It was simply too intense, too soul-shattering. She would never be free of him this way. Never be able to love another man, to be with another man if this is what she had to remember.

"Again," he said, before driving her once more to the peak.

When she came again, he crawled up her body, kissing his way over her sensitive skin. He was still wearing the riding boots, his black trousers open at the waist and hanging low on his hips.

Sydney could only stare. He was an erotic fantasy, a desert lover come to claim her. She was aching, quiver-

ing with need. The pale maiden ready for the possession of her dark lover.

"Do you want me, Sydney?"

"You know I do."

"That wasn't enough for you?" he asked silkily.

She shook her head against the pillows. She knew
she must look wild, her hair plastered to her head from
the shower, her skin flushed with the glow of amazing
sex. But she didn't care.

She needed him inside her. Needed him to breathe.

He urged her up, turned her so that she was facing
away from him on all fours. He stroked her sex, kin-
dling the flame again until she was panting with need.

And then he plunged into her. Sydney arched backward, her hair fanning across her back. Malik wrapped
an arm around her waist, held her against him as he
thrust into her body. His other hand found her, moved
expertly against her slick flesh.

It was raw, earthy, and she loved it. He could have
taken her gently, reverently, but instead he'd taken her
with all the power and wildness he possessed.

It wasn't fairy tale lovemaking—but she didn't want
fairy tale lovemaking. She wanted *this*.

This raw need that scorched her from the inside out.
That branded her as a sexual being who craved the kind
of release that only this man could give.

She came again in a hot, hard rush, collapsing against
him while he held her steady and pumped into her body.
This time, he followed her, his body stiffening as he
moaned her name.

She loved the sounds he made when he was stripped
of his control, the way his body jerked and shuddered.
She did that to him. It made her feel powerful, needed.

His fingers stroked along the column of her spine,

his touch reverent. He collapsed onto his back, and she turned so that she could face him. He reached up to push away a hank of her hair that had fallen across her face, and then cupped the back of her head and pulled her down for a lingering kiss.

"You've destroyed me," he murmured.

But what she was thinking was that he'd destroyed her. It didn't matter what happened, how many days they spent together, whether they made love or studiously avoided touching one another—she felt something for this man that was never going to dissolve. Time and distance hadn't managed it so far, though she'd convinced herself that it had.

Tears pricked the backs of her eyes. One afternoon in his arms, and the truth was too blinding to ignore.

CHAPTER ELEVEN

WHEN Malik awoke, the tent was dark. He moved his foot, grateful that he'd at least managed to get out of the riding boots at some point. Beside him, Sydney was curled into a small ball. He lifted onto an elbow, smiled as he gently drew her curtain of hair from her face. He'd always loved the way she slept.

She lay on her side, her body curled as tight as it could be, as if she were trying to make herself smaller. He frowned for a moment. It was very much like Sydney to try and make herself disappear. He'd known, when they were together, that she often tried to go unnoticed.

She truly believed that she was without any remarkable qualities, which he found both interesting and baffling. He'd never known a woman who was more remarkable, or more certain she was not.

He stretched and climbed from the bed naked, in search of the food they'd left on a table nearby. It was cold in the desert at night, but he was still too hot to bother covering up. He found flat bread and olives, a bit of cheese. He didn't need much, but he needed something if the way his stomach was growling was any indication.

Sydney didn't stir. And no wonder. It was a mystery that he could.

His body was sated, content—his mind was not. He thought back to that moment in the shower when she'd taken him in her mouth. He'd nearly come apart then and there, but somehow he'd managed to keep it together long enough to regain control of himself.

He felt a moment's guilt for the way he'd taken her once they'd made it to the bed. But he'd been so on edge, so unsure of himself and so raw with the wounded feelings he'd buried down deep that he couldn't lie in her arms and spill himself into her body with her soft limbs wrapped around him and her cries in his ear.

He'd needed to take her like an animal, needed that slight disconnect that turning her away from him would give.

Except that he'd failed rather spectacularly. Because it didn't matter how he made love to Sydney, she still managed to crack him wide open until his feelings were so raw that he wasn't sure how to deal with them.

When he'd recovered sufficiently, he'd dealt with them by taking her again, this time as they entwined their bodies together, limbs tangling, hands clasping, tongues dueling for supremacy. Her cries of ecstasy fueled some hidden fire in his gut that only made him want to push her further and further over the edge.

Malik pushed a tired hand over his eyes, rubbed his arm against his face. It had been a very long afternoon, punctuated by bouts of sleeping combined with the sort of lovemaking that turned him inside out each and every time. He didn't care to examine why, though he knew he would have to at some point.

All he knew was that Sydney was a fire in his body like no other woman had ever been. He was addicted to the rush he felt whenever he was inside her, addicted to the way she made him feel better than he'd ever felt in his life. With her, he felt...right.

Somewhere during it all, they'd managed to eat.

He'd told her last night she would be his wife again. He didn't know precisely why he'd done it, except that he'd been angry with her for being so determined to push him away again. She'd walked out on him once, and he'd been too proud to go after her. He should have done.

He should have chased her all the way to L.A. and reminded her why they were so good together.

But she was here now, and he wasn't going to let her go again without making very sure she understood precisely what she would be giving up.

"Malik?"

"Over here," he said. "Do you want something to eat?"

She pushed herself up in the bed and yawned. "No thanks. What time is it?"

Malik shrugged. "I'm not sure. I haven't checked. It's probably earlier than it should be."

"What do you expect? We did sleep part of the day away."

"Is that what we did?" he asked, making his way back to the big bed and the warm woman waiting for him.

She laughed. "Sometimes."

"How are you feeling?"

She lifted her arms in a sensual stretch. "Tired. Sore."

He'd hoped she would say *happy*. He told himself not to care that she did not.

"Perhaps we should have taken it slower," he said instead.

"I'm not sure that was possible."

No, probably not. He'd never been very good at maintaining his control with her. "Nevertheless, you almost succumbed to heat stroke. I should have been more careful."

She shook her head. "And yet here I am, remarkably alive and unaffected by your callous treatment of me."

He tried not to laugh. It didn't work. "I should love to treat you callously more often."

She sighed. He didn't like the wistfulness he heard in the sound. Something was coming that he'd prefer to leave alone for the time being. He was not, however, going to get his wish.

"It was beautiful, Malik. Wonderful and amazing, as always. But how does sleeping together help the situation?"

Her words pricked him. He had no idea what happened next, how making love to her fit into his life beyond this very moment, and he didn't want to think of it. They'd had an extraordinary day together, getting to know each other's bodies again, feeling the emotion that burned between them as they did so.

Being inside Sydney wasn't just about sex. He knew that, but he didn't know what else to call it. How to say it. He knew she was determined to move forward with the divorce, determined they could not build a life together, and he couldn't think of one good reason why she was wrong.

Except that it *seemed* wrong somehow. Why couldn't they figure it out? Why couldn't they take it a day at a time and try to build something more lasting?

"It helps me feel calm," he said lightly, because he wasn't prepared to take the conversation any deeper.

She blew out a breath. "Does it make you feel any-thing else?" she asked, her voice smaller than it had been.

He pulled her to him then, stretched out over top of her, his mouth finding the sweet skin of her throat. "You know it does, Sydney."

Her fingers slipped over his shoulders, a small moan issuing from her as he licked the flesh of her neck and then blew softly on the wet spot. "But I *don't* know it," she said. "I have no idea what you feel. All I know is we have this amazing chemistry in bed together. But that's not enough, is it?"

"It's a start." He didn't want to talk about feelings, not right now. The idea of it created a hard knot of tension deep in his belly. "Why question our good fortune?"

He palmed her breast, tweaked a nipple as she gasped. "Malik," she breathed. "This is serious."

"I know. Very serious." He claimed her lips, delved inside with his tongue. She kissed him ardently, her hands threading into his hair as her body arched.

He was growing hard again. He knew the moment she realized it, because she gave a little moan. And then she tilted her hips up and ground them against him.

"Temptress," he said, and then he bent his head and took the hard bud of her nipple into his mouth.

"Oh—I can't think when you do that."

"Then don't think. Feel."

"But Malik," she said on a half groan. "I want to talk to you. I want to know you. I want more than just this."

He lifted his head. Irritation was growing inside him. Frustration. And a sense of panic that was completely foreign to him. "I ache for you, Sydney. I've ached for a year. Is this not enough for you?"

She didn't say anything for a long moment. "No," she said. "It's not enough."

Malik rolled away from her with a groan. He put his arm over his face, covering his eyes. His body throbbed, but that was nothing compared to the piercing throb of his heart.

"We've been down this path before," she said. "And look where it got us."

Malik sat up and began to hunt for his trousers. "If you will remember, *habibti*, you ran away." He knew he sounded cold, but he had to. It was that or cave in to the hot emotion in the air—and he wasn't ready for that. He would never be ready for that.

"I did run. And maybe I was wrong, but you share some of the blame, too."

"Yes, I know this." He found the trousers, shoved a leg in first one side and then the other before standing and pulling them up to fasten them.

"That's it?" she said. "You're leaving? You'd rather have sex or walk out than talk to me?"

She sounded bitter. And angry.

"Right now, yes."

She got to her knees in the middle of the bed. He tried not to look at the way the dim light from the lamps limned the silky skin of her breasts. The way it kissed her curves, disappeared in the shadowed cleft between her thighs. She put her hands on her hips, and his gaze shot up to her face, more for self-preservation than anything else.

"You're unbelievable, you know that? You talk about me running away, but what about you? You can't face any conversation that might be about the way you feel."

He stood there, clenching his fists at his sides. Willing himself to be calm and methodical about this. He thought back to his childhood, to those days when he'd longed for someone—*anyone*—to tell him he was loved, valued. Wanted for more than dynastic reasons. For more than reasons that were only about tradition and duty.

His father was proud. He cared for his children in his own way, but he wasn't demonstrative. And his mother...

Malik frowned. His mother had no maternal feelings whatsoever. Children were a duty, something one produced before handing them over to be raised accordingly. She only became interested in him when he was old enough to do what he wanted without recourse.

He'd never talked about his feelings because there was nothing to talk about. No one to talk about them with. Since he'd become a man, he'd heard those three words often—*I love you*—but always from women whose motives he did not trust. Women who wanted to trap him for his wealth and position, not for who he was at heart.

And who was he, really? What great prize was he?

Malik ground his teeth in frustration. "Our relationship didn't break down overnight. I don't imagine it can be fixed overnight, either."

"Relationship? Is that what you call this? I thought it was just sex."

"What do you want from me, Sydney? We've been apart a year. Do you expect a declaration of true love?"

"No," she cried quickly. Too quickly. "That's not what I want. Not what I expect."

And yet he knew she did. She was a woman who was open with her feelings, even when she thought she wasn't. Her every emotion was written on her face. He couldn't be like her, even if he wanted to. He was too used to protecting himself, denying himself.

What happened if he tore down the walls between him and the world? "I'm not sure I can be what you expect," he said. "I can only be what I am."

"How do you know what you can do," she said sadly, "if you won't even talk about it?"

The next morning, Malik announced they were leaving. Sydney looked up from the tray Adara had just brought in for them, her heart sinking into her stomach.

"But we've only just arrived. I thought you had business to conduct."

Malik's handsome face was studiously blank. "I've done what I needed," he said. "We're moving on to the city of Al Na'ir. You will be more comfortable there."

"And by done what you needed, do you mean enticing me into your bed again?" It was the wrong thing to say, but she couldn't seem to stop herself.

His jaw looked harder than granite. "That was so very difficult to do, wasn't it? No, Sydney, that is not what I mean."

She lifted her chin. No, it hadn't been difficult, just like it hadn't been difficult when she'd met him last year.

"Be ready in an hour," he said. She thought he looked as if he would say something else, but instead he turned and went back outside. Sydney balled her hand into a fist and punched one of the cushions on the couch.

She had no one to blame but herself. She'd known what being with Malik again would mean, and she'd fallen headlong into hedonism anyway.

Her body was still languorous from their intense lovemaking of yesterday. She'd lost track of how many times they'd awakened from a nap to sink into each other again. It had been a day of excess, of pleasure so intense she'd wanted to weep from it.

It had also been a day in which she'd realized that nothing had changed for her. She was still in love with Malik. She'd pushed him to talk, but it hadn't quite been fair of her. Only a few days ago, he'd told her about Dimah, about his family and his relationship with them when she'd asked.

Compared to what they'd talked about before, it had been a lot of revelations in a short span of time. Malik did not open up easily. She knew that, but she'd been feeling so vulnerable after realizing how she still felt about him.

She'd wanted to know he was affected, too. That some part of him wanted more than just sex. The way he'd touched her in the shower, his hand trembling—it had to mean something, didn't it? And after, when he'd been so focused on her pleasure, so determined to make her feel good—what had he said? *I have not forgotten even a moment of making love to you.*

Even now, the words had the power to make her shiver.

She'd been certain he must feel *something*—but Malik was not the sort of man to talk openly about his feelings. He never had been. Sydney bit her lip. She had no idea where things stood between them now. Just because they'd had sex, it didn't mean that everything was grand.

It didn't mean they could leave Jahfar and forget about the divorce. Nor did she want to. She'd given up everything when she'd married him—and then she'd given up her self-respect while she'd waited for him to say he loved her, to contradict what he'd told his brother on the phone.

She would not be so weak again. Loving someone didn't mean you were capable of having a relationship with them, especially if they didn't have the same level of commitment to it as you.

Sydney gathered her things together and shoved them into the small suitcase she'd brought. It wasn't very hard to do so since she hadn't brought a lot. Within the hour, they were in the Land Rover and heading out of the oasis. Sydney turned to look back at the stand of palms with the cool, clear water and the black goat-hair tents arrayed around it. A child stood behind one of the palms, arms wrapped around the tree, watching them go.

Inexplicably, hot tears rose to her eyes. Not because she was going to miss the oasis terribly—she hadn't been there long enough to get attached to it—but the child represented a kind of innocence she would never have again. It was impossible not to be tossed about by the vicissitudes of life when you got older. And impossible not to long for a simpler time when your heart was breaking.

Sydney blinked away the tears as she turned to concentrate on the rolling sand before them. The desert was blinding, but the windows were tinted and helped to cut the glare. Waves of heat rippled in the distance. Malik had the air on, but only barely. She knew it was to keep the engine from overheating.

"How long will it take?" she asked.

Malik shrugged. "About two hours."

They lapsed into silence then. Sydney stared out the window, but her eyes were growing heavy. She hadn't had nearly enough sleep last night. She tried to keep them open, but finally gave up to the inevitable and dozed off.

She awakened with a start, what felt like only a short time later. Something didn't feel quite right. She blinked, sitting up higher. And then she realized—

The Land Rover wasn't moving. And Malik wasn't inside any longer.

In a panic, she grabbed for the door pull and yanked hard. The vehicle sat at an angle that tilted her door down so that it swung wide very quickly when the latch was released.

Sydney barely caught herself before she tumbled onto the sand below.

"Careful," Malik said, and her thudding heart gave a little leap. He hadn't left her.

She closed her eyes. Dear God, she wasn't alone.

"Why did we stop?" she asked, climbing down from the vehicle to join him.

The Land Rover sat in the minimal shade of a giant dune. She glanced up, realizing the sun was still fairly high overhead. It was past its zenith, which meant it was after the noon hour at least.

She brought her gaze back to Malik, her pulse thrumming quickly, her blood pumping hard. She didn't know if it was fear, or the adrenaline from nearly falling into the sand.

Malik leaned against the side of the Land Rover. His head was wrapped and his dark gaze burned steadily as he stared at her.

This couldn't be good....

"We did not stop on purpose, *habibti*. We have broken down."

CHAPTER TWELVE

THE hours passed slowly in the desert. Sydney gazed up at the horizon for the hundredth time, wondering where their rescue was. Malik had told her not to fear because he had a satellite phone and a GPS transmitter. They were not lost, and not unrecoverable.

But they were all alone, and likely would be for some hours yet. There had been a sandstorm to the north, which cut them off from Al Na'ir city. And Al Na'ir city from them.

A hose had broken, and there was no spare. Malik seemed calm enough now, but she knew he would have sworn violently when he realized it.

Yet he'd let her sleep through the whole thing.

Sydney perched on a chair in the sand and made whorls with her foot. It was hot, but not as bad now that the sun had fallen deeper and deeper in the sky. The shadow of the dune was long, and they were in it. Thankfully.

"Drink some water," Malik said, handing her a fresh bottle from the cooler in the back. Not that the water was icy cold, but it had been refrigerated in the oasis and put into a chilled container for their trip.

Sydney unscrewed the top and took a sip. "Will they

come soon?" she asked, wiping her hand across her mouth.

Malik looked toward the horizon. Then he turned back to her. "The truth is that I don't know. It may be morning before anyone can make it."

"Morning?" She tried not to shudder at the thought. A night in the desert. In a Land Rover. Not exactly her idea of a fun vacation.

Malik shrugged. "It will be fine. So long as the storms don't turn south."

"And if they do?"

He speared her with a steady look. "That would be bad, *habibti*. Let us hope they do not."

A few minutes of silence passed between them again. "Malik?"

He turned to look at her. He was every inch a desert warrior, she realized. Tall, commanding and as at home in this harsh environment as he was in the finest tuxedo. "Yes?"

"Did you spend much time in the desert when you were growing up?"

She thought he might not answer, might consider it too personal in light of their conversation last night, but he nodded slowly. "My father thought that his boys should all understand and fear the desert. We came many times, and when we reached a certain age, we underwent a survival test."

She didn't like the way that sounded. "A survival test?"

He took a drink of his own water. "Yes. We were left at a remote location with a survival pack, a compass and a camel and told to find our way to a certain point. None of us ever failed."

"But if you had?"

"None of us did. If we had, I imagine my father would have sent someone to retrieve us before we died."

Sydney swallowed. She couldn't imagine such a thing. How could you send your own children into danger?

"I don't understand your life at all." It was so foreign to her, so otherworldly. She'd been protected, educated, guided. She'd never been tested.

Perhaps she should have been. If she had been allowed to choose for herself, even if the choice was wrong, then maybe she'd have learned to trust herself more.

"And I don't understand yours," he replied.

She took a deep breath. "Then tell me what you want to know about me. I'm an open book, Malik." Because, if she were open with him, if she were willing to talk, then maybe he would do the same. Maybe they could learn to understand each other. It was a long shot, but she had nothing left to lose.

His gaze grew sharp. Considering. "I want to know why you have no confidence in yourself, Sydney."

Her stomach flipped. "I don't know what you mean. That's ridiculous."

"You do. You work for your parents, at a job you despise, and you think you are not worthy of more. They've taught you that you are not worthy of more."

"I don't despise my job." But her throat was dry, her ears throbbing as the blood pounded in them. "And my parents only want the best for me. That's all they've ever wanted."

She'd attended the finest schools, taken culture and deportment lessons, learned to ride horses, play piano. Her parents had given her everything she needed to be successful.

They were wildly successful, a perfect couple—and their children would be perfect, too. The perfect Reed family.

"You do despise your job," he said firmly. "You're good at it, but it's not what you want."

Her eyes burned. "How do you know what I want?"

"Because I pay attention. You don't miss your job when you are away. You would rather play with your designs on the computer."

Her pulse was racing, throbbing, aching. "How do you know that? I've never told you that."

"Because I know more than you think, Sydney."

She could only stare at him, wondering. And then it dawned on her.

"You had me watched," she said, her throat suddenly threatening to close up. "You spied on me."

His gaze glittered. "I did have you watched. For your safety, *habibti*. You are my wife, and just because you chose to leave me, that did not mean you would not be of interest to people."

She couldn't believe what she was hearing. And yet it suddenly made terrible sense. She'd always wondered why no one ever bothered her, why the paparazzi left her alone. She was the wife of a renowned international playboy, and no one ever hounded her for pictures or quotes.

She should have known. Anger welled inside her. "You had me watched, but you never called me yourself."

"I have already stated it was so."

"I realize that," she snapped. "It just sounds so unbelievable, even for you. As if picking up the phone and calling me was such a monumental task."

"We have discussed this before," he said evenly. "The answer has not changed since the last time."

Sydney crossed her arms and looked out over the red desert. So much time wasted, and all because of pride. *Both of you*, a little voice said.

"You made sure no one bothered me, didn't you? The paparazzi, I mean."

"Yes."

She thought of the media in L.A., the way they hounded the stars, the way nothing ever seemed to stop them from getting one more picture, a picture they hoped would be embarrassing or shocking enough to earn them big money on the open market. She wasn't a celebrity, but he was. She would have definitely been on their radar for her connection to him alone.

But for Malik's intervention. He should not have been able to do it. But he had.

"How?"

"Money is a strong motivator, Sydney. And power. Never forget power."

She looked down, at the whorls her foot was making in the sand. Emotion threatened to choke her, but she would not let it. He had done it for his own purposes, not for her. She couldn't think it was more than it was.

"Well, okay then." She sucked in a breath, and then another. "But what makes you think I have no confidence? I meet with clients as wealthy as you on a regular basis. And I've sold a lot of real estate. You can't do that without confidence."

"Tell me about your family," he commanded.

She looked at him askance. "Why? What's that have to do with this discussion."

"Humor me."

She folded her hands in her lap, her emotions in riot.

"What is there to tell that you don't already know? My parents are passionate about their real estate business and they've built it into one of the most successful firms in L.A. My sister is incredibly smart. She'll take over the business one day, and she'll make it into something even better than it already is."

"And you?"

She ran her tongue over her lower lip. "I'll help her."

"Help." He said it as a statement, not a question. "Why don't you take over? Or why don't you be her partner?"

Sydney rolled her neck. She was beginning to feel like this was the inquisition. And she wasn't enjoying it, regardless that she'd said she was an open book. Apparently she was not so open as she claimed. "I *will* be her partner. That's what I meant."

"But not what you said."

"And your point would be?" She arched an eyebrow, tried her best to look haughty. Hard to do when you were sweaty and tired.

"My point is that you can't think of yourself in control. You think your sister is the better business-woman—"

"Because she is," Sydney said. "There's no shame in admitting it." Not that it didn't prick her sometimes to think she wasn't the one her parents counted on, but that's just how it was. She was valuable in her own way.

"You told me once that you wanted to study graphic design and art."

"I did?"

"In Paris. Shortly after we were married. We went to dinner at that little café on the Seine, and you told me you had always wanted to design things for people. Websites, logos, advertising."

She remembered now, remembered that night when she'd been drunk on love and tipsy from too much wine. Her entire life had seemed to be waiting for her, a long stretch of time in which everything would be perfect because she'd married her own Prince Charming. She'd felt nervous and she'd wanted to impress him, because she was beginning to realize the import of what she'd done when she'd married him. He was not simply a man who happened to have a title. He was a prince in all senses of the word.

He'd made her feel insignificant, though he'd not said a word to make her feel that way. It was his presence, his bearing. The knowledge that she was out of her depth and would no doubt lose her appeal once he realized how very boring she was.

"There's nothing wrong with that," she said. "Graphic design is a legitimate business."

He scoffed. "That's your father talking, trying to form you into something he can understand. Something he can approve of." His voice dropped. "But that's not what you really want, Sydney."

Her heart was pounding, threatening to leap from her chest. Sweat beaded on her skin, and not from the heat. Her palms were clammy as she wiped them down the fabric of her *abaya*.

"I honestly don't know what you're talking about—"

He moved then, grabbed her by the shoulders and bent so that his face was only inches from hers. "I've been inside your apartment. I've seen the paintings on your walls that have your signature. And I watched you in the Louvre, the Jeu de Paume, the Orangerie. You want art, Sydney. Beautiful, magical art. It's what you want to do, whether it's to paint or to simply own a gallery

of your own where you showcase collections you have
selected—"

"No," she cried, pushing him away. "You're wrong!"

"Am I?"

She could only stare up at him, her body hurting with
the truth of what he said, her mind rebelling. It was so…
crazy. There was no money in such a thing, no future.
The paintings on her wall were from a different time in
her life, when she'd still thought she might find a way
to do what she wanted. They had been part of that cul-
tural education she'd received: enough to educate, but
not enough to corrupt.

But she was no one, nothing. How could she dare to
paint, dare to claim she knew art well enough to run
a gallery?

Her parents would be horrified. Alicia would frown
and shake her head. Sydney, flighty Sydney, off on one
of her fantastical mind trips again. Being an imperfect daughter. A disappointing daughter. An *ungrate-
ful* daughter.

She put her face in her hands and took deep breaths.
She would not cry. It was ridiculous to cry. Who got
upset over such a thing? Lots of people worked jobs
they hated in order to pursue the hobbies they loved
on the side.

Except that she'd even denied herself that. She'd
never pursued art, as if it were an abomination to do so.

No. She'd never pursued it because once she started,
she was afraid of where it would lead. Of the obsession
it might become.

The Reed Team needed her. Her parents. Alicia.
They counted on her.

But if that were true, a voice asked, why had she

left them so easily when Malik had asked her to the first time?

"Sydney." His voice was soft, his hands gentle on her arms. He pulled her palms from her face.

She sniffled. "It's a fantasy, Malik. I can't afford to be a starving artist. I don't even know what I would paint."

He smiled then, his hand sweeping wide. "What about this? The dunes are beautiful, are they not?"

"They are." She gripped his arm. "But I haven't painted in years. I'd be terrible."

"Does it matter?"

Did it? Was this really something she could do?

"I—I guess not." What did being terrible matter so long as you enjoyed it? Lots of hobbyists would never be professionals, but that didn't stop them from enjoying their hobbies. "So long as I don't quit my job," she added. She tried to smile, but it shook at the corners.

"Was that so hard to admit? You aren't doing what makes you happy, Sydney. You're doing what makes other people happy. You have to put yourself first for once. Stop caring what they think."

"You make it sound so easy. But it's not, Malik. I still have responsibilities." And the expectations that went with those responsibilities.

"You also have a responsibility to yourself."

Sydney gazed up at the sky. It was growing darker now, and much more quickly than she'd thought it would. "Do you always put yourself ahead of your responsibilities?"

"This is not what I said. You confuse the matter." He took a drink of water from the bottle he held. She watched the slide of his throat, her body heating irrationally as she did so. Everything he did was sexy, and she was like an addict looking for her next fix. It irritated her, especially now.

"What about your arranged marriages? Those were a responsibility, weren't they?"

He leveled his gaze at her. His expression was troubled, but he quickly masked it. "They were. The second one does not trouble me. But the first…"

He shook his head. "I failed miserably when I blamed Dimah for forcing me into it. It wasn't her fault. It was our parents, our tradition. Not her. And if I hadn't been so cruel to her, if I had married her without the bitterness, she would be alive today."

Sydney felt rotten for bringing it up. Why had she done so?

She knew why. Because she was feeling raw, exposed and maybe even a little bit confused. He'd held her over the coals, and she'd wanted to strike back. Except that it wasn't nice. Or fair, in this case.

"I'm sorry, Malik. I shouldn't have brought it up."

He shrugged. "Why not? I have called you to task. It's your turn."

"Yes, but it's painful for you." And she didn't like being deliberately cruel.

He looked severe. "Only because a young girl died. If she had not, I would regret nothing of what I said to her. And I might have been selfish enough to walk out before the marriage was finalized. Or I might have married her and made her miserable."

Sydney sighed. "It's tragic what happened to her. But I can't believe it's completely your fault. Perhaps she was simply unstable. Perhaps she needed help and no one saw it."

"I'm not sure her death was intentional."

Horror threatened to close her throat. "What makes you think so?"

She didn't think he would answer, but then he finally sighed and spoke. "She sent me a text message earlier that day. She claimed she would do something drastic if I didn't call her."

"And did you?"

He turned his head away, gazing into the distance. And then he shot to his feet, his entire body vibrating with tension.

"What?" Sydney cried, standing and grabbing his arm. "What is it?"

The sky was darker than before. Toward the horizon it was purple—and the purple was growing, spreading upward. Sydney's bones liquefied. That wasn't right at all. Darkness spread from the top down once the sun was behind the horizon. But this…this was like the sky was being swallowed from the bottom up.

Malik turned then and pushed her toward the door to the Land Rover. "Get inside, Sydney. Roll up your window and close the vents."

She did as he instructed, her heart pounding with adrenaline. Malik got in beside her and began to do the same.

"It's a sandstorm, isn't it?" she said, turning to him. Shivering at the size and menace of the thing. She did not know what it was capable of, but she remembered that Malik had said it would be bad if the storm reached them.

He nodded, and then turned to look out the back window at the oncoming darkness. She followed his gaze, her heart sinking. The darkness was coming fast. The sky would soon disappear inside it.

"Will we die?" she asked, feeling suddenly very small.

Malik snapped toward her, his dark gaze hard, intense. Then he cupped her jaw and gave her a swift kiss. "No, we will not die. I promise you, Sydney."

CHAPTER THIRTEEN

"How can you promise that?" she cried.

His jaw hardened, his eyes glittering in the darkness. "Because I have seen this before. We will be fine. But we will be uncomfortable for a while."

She wasn't quite sure she believed him, but she desperately wanted to. Sydney turned to face the front of the car again. Bits of sand flecked against the paint, while ahead of them the sky was still clear. But it wouldn't last long. Soon, they would be buried in sand. Her heart lurched. She hoped they wouldn't *literally* be buried in sand.

Within fifteen minutes, she could barely see the Land Rover's hood. A trickle of sweat slid between her breasts. It was stifling in the confines of the SUV, but not unbearable. And she took comfort in knowing the temperature would cool dramatically in the next hour or so as the sun went down.

"Tell me what's the worst that could happen," she said.

He looked at her, his expression carefully neutral.

"I need to know, Malik."

He nodded. "We could be buried. The dune is close, and depending on the direction of the wind, it could blow onto us, covering us."

Her heart throbbed painfully. "And then what?"

"We try to dig out."

"Oxygen?"

"There are a few bottles packed away. Like hikers use at altitude," he explained.

"So we could survive a while."

"Yes."

Sydney shivered. She hoped it didn't come to that. But her heart wouldn't stop thudding, her stomach churning with dread. She turned to look out the windscreen again. The sand had swallowed them whole, and her stomach fell.

She put her fist to her mouth, chewed on her knuckle. It was an unconscious gesture, but when she realized what she was doing, she didn't stop.

"I called her," Malik said, drawing her attention once more. He sat with one hand on the bottom of the steering wheel, his head leaned back against the headrest.

She hadn't forgotten what they'd been talking about before the storm, but she hadn't thought he intended to answer the question. Though perhaps he was only trying to distract her from the storm. "You did?"

He rolled his head against the seat to look at her. Her insides squeezed at the expression on his face. He was still tormented by what had happened to Dimah. Though it hurt to see him this way, she knew there was nothing she could do to take away the pain.

"I did." His fingers flexed on the wheel. "And I was angry. I told her to stop being so dramatic. I told her there was nothing she could do to make me want our marriage."

Sydney reached out impulsively and put her hand on his. "I'm sorry. I know I keep saying it, but I don't know what else to say."

"There is nothing else to say. I was wrong, and I hurt her." He pressed a thumb and forefinger to his temples. "It was nearly ten years ago and I still feel guilty. I will always feel guilty."

The storm howled over them with even greater force then, stunning her and making her jump as she felt the strength of it against the SUV. Malik did not react, and she took some comfort from the fact. Perhaps it was nothing. When he looked worried, she would worry.

"I think that's very normal," she said, raising her voice to be heard over the wind. "If you didn't feel a little bit guilty, if you didn't think of her at all, you would not be the kind of man you are."

"And what kind of man is that, Sydney?"

She swallowed hard. What could she say? That he was the kind of man she could love? How would that help? "A good man. A man who cares that he hurt someone."

He reached out and caressed her cheek. Her skin prickled from his touch, a trail of fire following in the wake of his fingers. "I hurt you."

She dropped her gaze from his. "Yes."

"It's not what I wanted to do."

"It would have happened eventually," she said, her throat feeling tight.

His fingers stilled. "And what makes you say this?"

Could she tell him? The wind howled around them, the storm buffeting the Land Rover, blocking out most of the light, making her heart pound and her stomach clench. And she thought, *Why not? What is there to lose?*

And then, *We could die out here.*

But she would not die without saying what she needed to say.

She lifted her chin, looked him in the eye. She would not hide from him. Not now. "Because I loved you, Malik, and you did not love me."

There, she'd said it, and even if she hadn't quite said it properly, she'd told him what was in her heart. It was almost a relief to do so. And terrifying at the same time. What would he say?

He stroked her cheek again, his expression softer than she'd ever seen it. "I cared for you, Sydney," he said. "I still do."

Pain uncoiled a thorny tendril inside her. They could die tonight, no matter what he promised her, and that was all he felt. He *cared*.

It was something, she argued. Something more than he'd ever said before. And yet it left her feeling empty, sad.

"That's not enough," she finally said.

"It's what I have, Sydney. Feelings aren't…easy for me."

She put a hand to her chest, tried to hold in the hurt. "I *need* more. I want more. And if you can't—*couldn't*," she corrected, "give it to me, then I would have been hurt regardless of your intentions."

"I gave you everything I had," he said. "Everything I was capable of."

"Did you?" She laughed, but the sound was harsh. Bitter. "I think it's an excuse, Malik. I think you've spent a lifetime not feeling anything. That your upbringing made you afraid to feel because you were always afraid your feelings wouldn't be returned."

He looked furious—and he looked wild, hunted. As if he wanted to escape.

Knowing she was hitting so close to the mark only spurred her recklessly forward. "Your brother doesn't seem to have a problem with his feelings! Look at him with his wife—"

She stumbled to a halt, her emotions churning, her eyes pricking with angry, frustrated tears. Yes, look at King Adan with his wife. She would give anything to have what they had. She deserved that kind of love. Everyone did.

"My brother is not me." He sounded stiff, formal, and she recognized it for what it was: Malik retreating behind his walls.

"Don't you think I know that?" she cried. She sucked in a shaky breath. "I think you feel, Malik, but I also think you're still punishing yourself for Dimah's death, among other things."

His gaze glittered. "You have no idea, Sydney. You only think you do."

"Then why on earth don't you tell me?" she demanded, hot emotion threatening to overwhelm her. "Tell me, so I know what it is about me that's not good enough for you!"

The words hung in the air between them, heavy and pendulous. Neither of them moved or spoke for a long moment. She hadn't meant to say such a thing, and yet she'd been unable to stop the words from escaping.

Malik swore. And then he reached over and dragged her onto his lap. She pushed against him, tried to escape, but he held her with arms like bands of steel. Her belly was on fire—with shame, with anger, with unbelievable pain. It had hurt to say those words. And if she spoke again, even to tell him to let her go, she was afraid she'd burst into sobs.

Everything was racing out of control. The storm. Her feelings. Her reaction to him. She was tired and frustrated and angry and confused, and so many other things that she couldn't even name them all.

She wanted this to be easier. She wanted to love a man and have him love her in return. Normal. She wanted normal.

Temporarily defeated, Sydney turned her face into his chest, clutched him with her fist. Angry tears leaked down her cheeks.

Though she tried to hide it from him, Malik knew she cried. He reached up, caught a tear on his finger. "Have you ever thought," he said in her ear while she curled against him, silent tears dripping, "that maybe I am not good enough for you?"

Before she could answer, he tilted her chin back, claimed her mouth. Her mind whirled. She didn't intend to soften, didn't intend to kiss him back—but she did. It was inevitable.

What if they died tonight? What if the storm covered them and they never got out?

"You are good enough for a king, Sydney," he whispered harshly. "Never doubt it."

He pillaged her mouth, taking everything she would give him, and still demanding more. They kissed for what seemed like hours but was in fact only minutes. Sydney's body responded as it always did, softening, melting, her sex flooding with moisture and heat. She could feel Malik's response, his erection thickening beneath her thigh. She couldn't help but move against him. She loved to feel the answering hardness there, loved to hear his groan.

He tore his mouth from hers. "Do you want me, Sydney?" His voice broke at the end, a sound so needy and forlorn that it sliced through her defenses.

She'd never known him to sound so uncertain. "Yes," she answered. "Oh, yes."

He stripped her of her clothes until she sat in his lap in nothing but her bra and tiny lace panties. Then he buried his face in her cleavage, inhaling her scent, before slipping the cups off and teasing her breasts into merciless sensitivity. She threw her head back, thrusting her breasts forward for his pleasure.

"It's getting bloody hot in here," Malik said a few moments later.

"You're still wearing all your clothes."

"Indeed."

He managed to shrug out of the *dishdasha*, baring his gorgeous chest. His gaze on her body was so hot, so sensual, that she wondered how she didn't go up in smoke.

He slipped a finger beneath the waistband of her panties, found her wet and ready for him. But instead of removing her panties the usual way, he simply wrapped his fists in one side and tore them open with a swift tug.

"Malik!" It shocked her, that raw power. And thrilled her.

His eyes glowed in the gathering darkness. "I don't want to wait."

Neither did she. He freed himself from his trousers and then she was straddling him, sinking down on top of his glorious hardness. He filled her completely, made her shudder with sheer joy.

"There is nothing like this," he said, his chest rising and falling rapidly, as if he were holding onto control by the barest edge. "Nothing like being with you."

Then he gripped her hips and drove up into her, his thumb sliding across her sensitive bud in rhythm with his thrusts. Sydney threaded her hands into his crisp black hair, tilted his head back and fused her mouth to his, taking him the way he took her.

Relentlessly. Joyfully. Completely.

The pleasure spiraled higher and higher until she broke with it, coming in a long wave that held her in its grip far longer than she expected. It felt so good it almost hurt, and she cried out when it ended.

Malik was still so gloriously hard as he stroked her back with his fingers. "This is what happiness is," he said. "Being with you like this."

He'd never said as much before, but she wanted him to say more. He was as aware of the storm outside as she was, as worried that it might be their last time together. He had to be.

"Oh, Malik," she said. "Don't you understand it by now?"

In answer, he claimed her mouth roughly. And then he was driving into her again, stoking her body to incredible heights once more. At the last possible moment, he slipped his hand between them, found her again. Sydney flew over the edge with a cry that was torn from her throat.

A cry that sounded suspiciously like "I love you!"

Malik pulled her down to him, kissed her hard as he found his release in her body. His hips thrust into hers until he was spent, and then his kiss turned tender, gentle. As if he were a storm that had spent its fury and was now caressing the very land it had ravaged.

Sydney's pulse pounded in her ears. She knew what she'd said, what she'd been unable to keep inside. The emotion was so strong, buffeting her as much as the storm buffeting the Land Rover. She felt raw, exposed.

Malik pushed her damp hair from her face. "That was amazing," he said. "Thank you."

"Is that all?" she asked, her heart flipping in her chest, her throat aching from the giant knot forming inside.

His brows drew down. "What do you wish me to say, *habibti*?"

That was the moment, she thought, when her heart shattered into a million pieces. They were caught in a deadly storm, possibly permanently, and Malik felt nothing beyond supreme sexual satisfaction.

"Did you hear what I said to you?"

He swallowed, the only visible reaction. "I did. And I am happy for it." He stroked the underside of her breast. "But they are only words. Actions mean much more than words, don't you think?"

Sydney reared back. "The words are nice, too, Malik. Sometimes, the words are necessary."

"Anyone can say those words," he said. "It does not make them true."

"They are true for me."

He closed his eyes. "Sydney. Please, not now."

She climbed off him and gathered her clothes, hurriedly slipping into them again. "When? When is the right time? Or are you hoping we don't live through the night and then we never have to talk?"

His expression grew chilly. "Don't be dramatic."

"Dramatic? I said I love you and that's dramatic?" Her eyes stung with emotion. With pain. He wanted to marginalize her feelings for him and she hated it.

He jerked his trousers closed. "Do you want me to say I love you, Sydney?" His eyes flashed, his chest heaving as he stared at her. "Would that make you happy?"

He leaned forward and caught her chin, forced her

to look at him. "I love you," he said, though it came out as a growl. "Is that what you want to hear?"

She pushed his hand away and huddled near the door as the sand pelted the SUV. "No," she said to the glass. "Because you don't mean it."

His laugh was hollow. "And you said the words were important."

The storm howled for several hours, and the temperature dropped so that it was no longer so hot inside the Land Rover. A battery-powered lantern burned softly in the dark. Sydney stole a glance at Malik. He lay back against the seat, his eyes closed. His chest was still bare. But then so was hers, with the exception of her bra. It had been too hot to remain wrapped in her clothes, so she'd slipped the garment off again.

It was growing more comfortable now. Almost chilly.

Sydney reached for the fabric she'd discarded and slipped into it. Malik stirred then, his dark eyes snapping open as if he'd not been sleeping. He took in her form, and then peered out the window. She tried to pretend the lack of emotion in his gaze didn't bother her.

"The storm is nearly over," he said, his voice rough with sleep. "Soon, we may open the windows again."

"That's good," Sydney replied crisply, though she wouldn't feel any true relief until the air cleared and they could see the sky.

"You are okay?" Malik asked.

"I'm fine," she said, her voice a bit sharp.

He blew out a breath. "I'm sorry," he said. "I did not mean to hurt you."

Sydney shrugged. "It doesn't matter, Malik."

He subsided into silence again, and she felt hot and prickly all over. Not from heat, but from frustration and embarrassment. She'd confessed her stupid, naive feelings for him—and he'd thrown them back in her face. It mattered more than she would ever admit.

Sydney turned toward the window, pillowing her head on her hands, and closed her eyes. She hadn't been able to sleep yet, but maybe she would if she kept trying. She didn't feel like she had them closed for long before Malik spoke her name.

"Yes?" She blinked at him, yawning. Maybe she had slept after all.

"The storm has passed. I need to try your door, Sydney."

"My door?"

"Mine will not open. The sand is holding it closed."

Her anxiety spiked. What if they were trapped? Oh, God…

"Let me," she said firmly, needing to do something. "I'm right here."

He hesitated only a moment before nodding. "You must be careful. First, let the window down very slowly, just a fraction." He turned the key in the Land Rover, and she pressed the button. Thankfully, there was enough power to do the job. Sand flooded into the window the moment she had it open and she automatically pressed it back up again.

"No, let it down once more. If the sand lessens, that is a good sign."

"And if it keeps pouring in?"

"Then we have a problem," he told her. She liked that he didn't lie, but at the same time, she'd almost rather not know.

She pressed her face to the glass, shading her eyes. "But I can see darkness out this window. I think. If it were covered in sand, wouldn't I be able to see it?"

"Yes, but if the dune is unstable, it could collapse and send sand over us. What came in the window is from above. But I don't know how much is on top of us."

Great.

Sydney took a deep breath and tried the window again. The sand poured in once more, but it lessened very quickly until there was nothing more coming in. Though she was sitting, her knees wobbled.

"Roll it down farther and stick your hand out. Carefully. See if you can feel sand."

She did as he asked, reaching down and trying to touch the ground with her fingertips. "I don't feel anything."

Malik let out a breath. "Good. Now let me try. My arms are longer."

He leaned over her, his bare chest a fraction of an inch from her face. Sydney closed her eyes and tried not to breathe as Malik tested the sand. A moment later, he opened the door. Relief puddled inside her as it swung gently outward.

"We aren't trapped," she said. "But how is that possible when the sand was pouring in?"

"It came from the roof. Now climb out very carefully, then tell me what you see."

Sydney slipped out of the SUV. The ground was a lot closer than it had been, and she stumbled when she hit. The cold air washed over her, sending goose bumps crawling across her skin. Above, the sky was clear, the stars winking down in the billions.

But the Land Rover...

She shivered. "It's half-buried," she said. "Your side." And more than his side. Three quarters of it was hidden by sand, in fact. She could see where the sand had slid from the roof and into her window. It hadn't been a whole lot, she realized now, but it had seemed like it at the time.

Malik crawled out to join her. He studied the scene for a long moment. The Land Rover looked like one of those Michelangelo sculptures, the ones that were never finished and looked as if they were trying to break free of the rock. Only a portion of it showed—the passenger side—while the rest was buried beneath tons of sand.

"We were lucky, *habibti*," Malik said quietly.

She wrapped her arms around her body. "We could have died, couldn't we? If it had lasted just a while longer…"

He turned to her, his expression fierce. "It did not. And we are well."

"The power of it," she marvelled. It was staggering. She was trapped in the middle of a vast desert with Malik. They were so small, so inconsequential. Their problems were nothing out here.

"The desert is not a place for amateurs."

She huffed in a breath. "Doesn't it bother you at all? That we could have died?"

"We did not," he said roughly. "And we will not. I promised you that."

"Don't you *feel* anything?" Angry tears sprang into her eyes and she dashed them away with the back of her hand.

He was looking at her, his expression sadder than she'd ever seen it. "Yes. I feel regret, Sydney."

Her blood slowed in her veins. "Regret?"

"I should never have brought you to Jahfar."

Inexplicably, his words pricked her. "You had to. We have to be together until we can get the…the divorce," she finished, stumbling over the words.

He shook his head. His jaw was hard, his eyes bright. "I'm letting you go."

She was confused. "But the forty days—"

"A lie."

She looked at him as if he'd grown another head. "A lie?"

"An exaggeration," he said. "The law was a real one, but Adan and his government changed it in their reforms. It was written at a time when our society was more feudal, and it was intended to give some protections to women. A former queen talked her husband into writing the law when her sister was wedded, bedded and repudiated in the space of two days. I believe there was a war over the incident, in fact."

"Why?" she asked. She was beginning to tremble, but whether from the cold or from anger he couldn't say. "Why did you do it?"

He slashed a hand through the air. "Because I had to," he said. "Because you walked out on me and I was angry."

"You lied to get revenge?"

No, that was not at all what he'd done. But he couldn't say the words, no matter how he tried. He couldn't tell her that he'd needed her to come back to him. That he'd needed *her*.

Because it was dangerous to need people. If you needed people, they could wound you. Stab you in the heart.

"No, it was not revenge." He reached into the Land Rover to retrieve the satellite phone. It should work now that the storm had passed.

"I don't understand you," she said.

He turned to her. "I believe we have already established that we do not understand one another."

Her stormy eyes flashed. "I had to rearrange my entire life to come to Jahfar."

"You are my wife, Sydney. You agreed to do this when you wed me."

It wasn't a good enough reason, but nothing of what he'd done when he'd gone to Los Angeles had made sense to him at the time. He'd gone because he'd known she was meeting with an attorney.

But he had not known what he would do when he went to the house in Malibu that night.

"Yes, but that was before you called me a mistake! Before I knew that you wished you had not married me."

Malik hissed. Of all the stupid things he could have done, that had been right at the top, regardless that she'd never been meant to hear it. Because he knew she was the youngest child, that she felt like an underachiever next to her sister, and that she didn't believe in herself as much as she should. He'd known it all because she'd told him, whether she'd intended to or not.

She was strong and beautiful and loyal, and she usually put her family's needs and feelings before her own. She hadn't been accustomed to doing something solely for herself. He was convinced that marrying him in Paris had been the most rebellious thing she'd ever done.

Not that her parents had objected to that event. When they'd discovered their daughter had married a foreign prince, they'd been enthusiastic.

Too enthusiastic. He'd never told her, but they'd wanted to throw a huge party for her and Malik when they returned to California—and invite all their firm's clients. He'd put an end to that scheme, determined they would not use their daughter's marriage as an opportunity to pump up their business. If the party wasn't to celebrate Sydney's happiness, then it wasn't happening under his watch.

"I have explained this to you," he said stiffly. "I will not do so again."

Because it made him angry to think of it. Of what he'd said, of her listening outside the office door. It had not been his finest moment, even if his intentions had not been bad.

She swallowed hard and he knew she was determined not to cry. He did not make the mistake of thinking that she cried out of weakness. It was anger, pure and simple.

"You brought me out here for nothing," she said. "And worse, you made me—"

She pressed a hand over her mouth, turned away from him. He couldn't bear it, couldn't bear that he'd upset her. He grasped her shoulders, turned her into his arms. She balled up her fist and hit him in the chest, but it wasn't hard and he didn't let her go.

She hit him again, and he only held her tighter. She wasn't trying to hurt him. She was furious, hurt. And he deserved it. He deserved everything she did to him.

Her voice drifted up to him, muffled from where she'd pressed her face against his clothing. "You made me love you again, Malik. I would have been fine if you'd just given me a divorce and left me alone, but you had to drag me into your life again. I was almost free of you."

He stroked her hair, held her against his heart. "I am going to let you free. If it's what you still want."

Perversely, he hoped she would say no—but he'd given her no reason to do so. Even now, he couldn't seem to find the words to tell her he wanted her to stay.

She didn't say anything for a long moment. "Yes," she said, so softly he had to strain to hear. "Yes, it's what I want."

CHAPTER FOURTEEN

Los Angeles was a whirlwind of color, light and sound compared to the desert of Jahfar. She dreamed of the Maktal Desert sometimes, of the deep umber sand, sky like the finest sapphires and the blinding white sun.

But mostly she dreamed of a man. Sydney stood at her kitchen counter after a long day at work, eating takeout from a container and trying not to think about Malik. It wasn't working. She set the container down and put her head in her hands.

Why did she dream of Malik after all he'd done? It had been a month since she'd left Jahfar. He had called her once. They'd spoken for a few minutes, but the conversation was stiff and uncomfortable for them both.

When it had ended, she knew he wouldn't call again. She stared at her cell phone lying on the counter, considered calling him instead. She missed him, missed his smile, his seriousness, the way he held her and caressed her while they made love. The way he looked at her when he told her that happiness was being with her.

Sydney sniffed. She felt tight inside, as if she'd swallowed too many emotions that were fighting to get out. But she had to shut them down, didn't she? Because if she let herself feel the pain, she might lie in bed for the rest of her life.

It was going to take time. A lot of time.

She thought wistfully of the small artist set she'd bought in an art store over the weekend. She'd been too embarrassed to ask for help, as if she were doing something elicit, so she'd bought a kit that promised it contained all the paints and brushes she needed to get started.

She had yet to open it. It was tucked away in her guest room, her own guilty little secret.

Tonight. Tonight she would open it. She might not remember how to paint a tree or a flower, but she would try. At least she would try.

Art and work could coexist. Malik had been right that she needed to do something for her. That she needed to put herself first sometimes.

She'd done that when she'd left Jahfar, though it was the hardest thing she'd ever done.

She'd had no idea how quickly it would happen, but as soon as their rescuers had arrived in the desert, Malik had put her in one of the four cars and told the driver to take her to his home in Al Na'ir. She could still see his dark eyes, the way he'd looked at her when she'd climbed into the car that would take her away from him. He'd seemed resigned.

A second car had followed, but Malik stayed behind with the others. It was the last time she'd seen him. She'd bathed and changed in Al Na'ir, and then she was on a plane to Port Jahfar. Once there, Malik's private jet had whisked her out of the country before she could even catch her breath.

Her doorbell rang. The sound made her jump, her heart leaping into her throat.

Malik.

Was it possible? Had he come for her this time? She

pushed her hair from her face, straightened her skirt and hurried to the door, her heart pounding a million miles a minute.

But when she looked through the peephole, it wasn't Malik. Her sister stood on the other side, her head down so that Sydney couldn't see her face. Sydney undid the locks, disappointment spiraling inside her. She didn't really want to talk to anyone just now, especially not someone in a happy relationship.

But she couldn't pretend she wasn't home when it was her sister standing there. It wouldn't be right.

"Thank God you're here," Alicia said when Sydney pulled the door open.

Sydney blinked. Alicia was a mess. Her mascara ran down her face, her hair uncharacteristically mussed. Her entire body trembled, from the roots of her hair to the tips of her fingers. "Oh, my God, what happened?" Sydney exclaimed.

Alicia's lip quivered. "I—I just need to come in for a while. Can I?"

"Of course!" Sydney stepped back and let her sister in, then slotted the locks back into place. She hadn't been thinking straight since the moment she'd thought it might be Malik.

And seeing Alicia looking so upset had temporarily stunned her. Alicia was never anything less than poised.

Alicia went and sat on the couch. Then she doubled over and began to sob. Alarm raised the hairs on the back of Sydney's neck. She rushed to her sister's side and hugged her close.

"My God, Alicia, what is it? Did something happen to Jeffrey?"

That only made Alicia sob harder. Then she looked up and Sydney noticed it for the first time: Alicia's eye was red, as if someone had hit her. Soon, it would turn black and blue, but for now it was a blazing, ugly red.

A sharp feeling of panic sliced into her, turned her into a babbling idiot. "Honey, were you attacked? Should we call the police? Where's Jeffrey?"

Stop, a little voice said. *She needs you to be calm.*

It was shocking to think that Alicia needed her. But she did. Somehow Sydney managed to stop gibbering and simply hugged her tighter. "Just tell me when you're ready, okay?"

"It's Jeffrey," Alicia whispered a few moments later, her lip trembling. "He hit me."

The bottom fell out of Sydney's stomach. "He hit you? But he loves you so much!"

Alicia flinched. "He doesn't, Syd. He really doesn't. Jeffrey only loves himself." She stood and began to pace the room, shredding the tissue she'd dragged from her purse.

Sydney was having trouble processing everything— Alicia's eye, the ugly things her sister was saying—but she knew one thing for certain. "We need to call the police," she said firmly. Because no way in hell was that bastard getting away with this.

No way in hell!

"I can't," Alicia said, halting. Her eyes were wide, her lip trembling anew. "I can't. Everyone will think I'm so stupid. Mom and Dad will be so disappointed in me—"

Sydney shot to her feet and went to put an arm around her sister. "It's okay, Alicia. No one will think that. Everyone knows how smart you are."

Alicia's laugh contained a note of hysteria. "Sydney. Smart women don't stay with men who beat them."

Ice settled in the pit of her stomach. "This wasn't the first time?"

Alicia shook her head. "No."

"Sit down, tell me everything." Sydney guided Alicia to the couch and went to get her a cold drink from the refrigerator. Alicia was a health nut, but Sydney settled on a syrupy sweet soft drink with a slice of lemon anyway. Because sometimes you needed something sweet.

Alicia took the drink and sipped at it. They spent the next hour talking before Sydney persuaded her to go to the police. First she'd had to convince Alicia that she wasn't stupid, that men like Jeffrey were insidious. They took control subtly, and then not so subtly.

Sydney finally got Alicia down to the car and drove her to the police station.

It turned into a long night: the police interviewed Alicia, took her statement and swore out a warrant for Jeffrey's arrest. When it was done, Sydney brought Alicia back to her apartment and tucked her up in the guest room.

Sydney poured a glass of wine and sat on the couch. She was numb, absolutely numb. She'd been so wrong. About everything. She'd thought that Jeffrey was in love with Alicia, that the reason her sister never had time for lunches or girls' nights out or anything else was because she was so happy. But instead, Jeffrey had been controlling her. He flew into rages when she wasn't available to him. He had to know where she was at all times. He didn't want her to talk to anyone, not even her family. He was jealous of her time with anyone else.

And then he hit her. When his rage subsided, he cried and swore he would never do it again, that he loved her so much and would never hurt her.

Jeffrey spoke the words, but he did not mean them.

Words mean nothing. Actions do. That's what Malik had told her, what he believed.

Her heart throbbed with feeling. Maybe she'd been too stupid to see the truth. She'd been so focused on the words that she'd not paid as much attention as she should to the actions. Why had he taken her to Jahfar when it wasn't necessary in the first place?

She was still angry over that. Angry that he'd manipulated her. If he'd wanted to try to fix their relationship, why hadn't he just said so?

Sydney rubbed the back of her neck to try and ease the tension. *Had* he wanted to fix the relationship? Was that why he'd dragged her to Jahfar? Taken her out to the oasis?

Malik was an amazing man. Confident and sure, with the looks and the money to do whatever he wanted in life. Was he truly that insecure that he couldn't come out and say what he wanted from her?

Or maybe it wasn't insecurity. She thought of the night she'd gone to dinner at the palace. How formal and distant Malik and his brother were, like business associates rather than family.

And the next morning, when his mother had been in the dining room, berating him for marrying a foreigner. There'd been no feeling there, no connection other than a bloodline and the tolerance that went with that relationship. Malik did not like his mother as a person, though Sydney thought that he must be fond of her in some way. He'd defended her treatment of him as a child by pointing out that she'd been a child herself. A naive, lonely child who'd turned into a shallow and bitter woman.

Malik wasn't insecure. But he had, Sydney was certain, lacked love in his life. His mother was not the sort to hug her children and tell them she loved them.

Shame flooded her. What an idiot she'd been. She was too stubborn, too insistent on playing the wounded party. She ran away and then waited for a call that never came, convincing herself that she wasn't good enough. Wasn't important or special or loved. She was making it all about her when in fact it was about them as a couple. How they dealt with each other. How they understood—or failed to understand—each other.

She was behaving like a child, as Malik had accused her of doing. And she'd done it again that day in the desert when he'd told her he'd lied about the law. She'd been so hurt and betrayed that when he'd asked if she wanted to leave, she'd said yes. She'd paid no attention to the way he was holding her, to the fact he was actually admitting what he'd done and offering her freedom if that's what she wanted.

She still wasn't sure that meant he loved her, but it might be a start. And she was a fool for sitting here and nursing her wounded feelings when she should be calling him and trying to see if there was any way they could build something lasting together.

She loved him, damn it, and you didn't abandon the people you loved. Even when you thought they were abandoning you.

Love is not love, which alters when it alteration finds, or bends with the remover to remove.

Shakespeare had been a wise, wise man.

Sydney snatched up her phone and found Malik's number. Her finger trembled as it hovered over the call button. But then she punched it and waited as the connection was made, her heart hammering in her chest, her throat, her temples.

Please be there. Please.

But he wasn't. The phone rang several times before going to voice mail. Sydney hesitated, not knowing what to say. In the end, she clicked off the line without saying a word. Disappointment gnawed at her. She would call back. She would leave a message. But first she tried to compose what she should say, what sort of message she should leave for him.

The words wouldn't come.

Words mean nothing.

Sydney groaned. Just when they meant everything, at least to her, she couldn't find the right ones to save her life. Maybe Malik was right. Actions were more important.

The next few days were a blur. Sydney tried Malik a few more times, when she had a spare moment, but he never answered. Panic began to coil inside her. What if he was finished with her forever? What if his silence was deliberate?

Fortunately, her sister was doing better. Alicia had gone to their parents' home, more because they'd insisted than because she'd wanted to, and she'd gotten a restraining order against Jeffrey. Work was crazy without Alicia and their mother, who had stayed at home to dote on her daughter twenty-four hours a day.

Sydney's father was handling it well, but he'd been shell-shocked by the news. He still came to the office, but he seemed to need her to handle many more things than she ever had before. It was both surprising and frustrating. Surprising because she'd never realized how much he trusted her, and frustrating because she'd bought a ticket to Jahfar.

A ticket she was never going to use at this rate.

But within a week, Alicia and their mother were both back at work. Alicia's eye was covered with heavy makeup, but she moved as briskly and efficiently through her tasks as always. No one said anything about Jeffrey.

Sydney sat at her desk and clicked on an email from her mother. A potential new listing in Malibu. Her heart skipped a beat, but the address wasn't the same one as the home she'd sold to Malik. It was two doors down. She thought about going to her mother's office and asking if someone else could take the appointment, but she decided against it. She would get through today, and then she would catch the late flight to Jahfar.

She simply couldn't put it off another minute. The Reed Team was a well-oiled machine, even if they'd had a hiccup recently. Her father had relied on her, and she was grateful, but it hadn't been necessary. The other agents and lawyers took up the slack and made everything run efficiently. She could escape for a few days at least.

When she told Alicia what she was planning, her sister merely hugged her and wished her good luck.

"You don't mind if I go?" Sydney asked.

"Of course not." Alicia squeezed her hand. "I'm fine, and I want you to go. Go get that prince of yours before some other woman snaps him up."

Sydney shuddered at the thought.

"But you are going out to Malibu later, right?" Alicia asked from the door of Sydney's office. "I don't think anyone else is available, and Mom says it's an important listing."

"I'm going," Sydney said. "There's enough time."

Alicia seemed relieved. "Good."

Once Alicia was gone, Sydney's mind began to race

with everything she needed to do before she boarded the plane tonight. She had a meeting with a client at three, and then she would drive to Malibu. Once she toured the home and took the listing details, she'd have just enough time to dash home and throw some things together before heading to the airport.

Her stomach churned. What if Malik wasn't in Jahfar? She had no idea whether or not he was, but she knew where he lived and she knew that when she arrived he would be alerted. And then he would return, and she would tell him she was a fool.

And she would pray it wasn't too late.

Around five-thirty, Sydney parked her car in the driveway of the Malibu home. The house Malik had bought was just up the street. She'd passed it coming in. There'd been no activity, no cars in the drive. Not that she'd expected there would be. She fully expected Malik would sell the home in the next few months.

But it did have a gorgeous view. It was the kind of home she'd have bought if she'd had Malik's money. A dream home. She could almost picture the two of them enjoying the sunset…and then enjoying each other. A flash of heat rocketed through her at the thought. Right now, the possibility of being with Malik again seemed remote and unreal.

But she was determined to try.

Sydney grabbed her briefcase and straightened her skirt before walking up the stairs to the door. She'd chosen a long sea-green sundress today and paired it with a white bolero sweater and low-heeled sandals. She would have to change into something a bit warmer for the long flight to Jahfar.

Excitement bubbled in her veins. And fear. What if Malik turned her away? What if he was through dealing with a childish wife? What if he was the one who wanted to move on now?

Sydney shook her head. No, she would not think like that. She would take the frightening leap and let everything happen as it may.

Sydney punched the doorbell, pasting on her best smile as she did so. The door jerked open. A dark-haired man stood in the entry, his presence making her nearly jump out of her skin.

She blinked, certain she wasn't seeing him right. But no, he looked like Malik. Except he wasn't Malik. He was tall, golden-skinned. His chiseled features were familiar, and not familiar. Handsome, like an Al Dhakir male.

Her heart began to pound.

"Hello, Sydney," he said in a distinctly Jahfaran accent. "I am Taj."

"I…" She swallowed, blinked again. He must have thought she was an idiot. "I'm pleased to meet you," she said at last, though her throat was as dry as the Maktal Desert.

Taj smiled. He was, of course, breathtaking. "I have heard a lot about you," he said, golden-voiced, golden-skinned, golden-smiled.

"You have?"

"Naturally. My brother talks of little else."

She stopped in the spacious entry. Tears of relief pricked the corners of her eyes as her pulse thundered out of control. "Malik? Is he here?"

Taj tucked her hand into his arm and started toward the terrace. "Why don't you come and see for yourself?"

Taj led her across a cavernous living room decorated all in white and onto the terrace. A profusion of flowers bloomed in containers, their bright colors framing the golden beauty of the man standing near the pool. Behind him, the ocean glistened in the late afternoon sun. Seagulls swooped in the distance, their piercing cries carrying on the currents.

Sydney's heart turned over. Malik wore a tuxedo, of all things, and his hands were shoved into the pockets of his trousers. She wanted to rush into his arms, and yet she was paralyzed. She'd tried to find him for days, and here he was. Right here. So close to her and yet so far.

"If you will excuse me," Taj said, "I must change clothes."

Sydney nodded, but her throat had closed up and she couldn't speak. Words, how silly. Who needed words? She couldn't think of anything to say, even if she could manage to force the words out.

Malik's gaze flickered behind her. He nodded once, and then focused his attention on her again. His dark eyes were hot, intense. She loved the way he looked at her. She loved him.

But did he love her?

And yet she was so relieved he was here, because she hadn't been sure she would actually see him again. What if he'd turned her away without seeing her first?

But here he was. Her beloved. Her handsome, handsome husband. Emotion welled in her.

He crossed the distance between them and stopped. She'd thought he was going to put his arms around her, but they remained at his side. She ached for him to touch her, to speak. Her skin was so tight, so confining. She wanted to slip into him, become a part of him.

She wanted his heat and his power the way she'd had it in the desert. Her dress suddenly felt too hot, in spite of the breeze coming off the ocean. She wanted to strip. Right here, right now. She wanted so many things, and she had no idea where to start—or if he'd want to hear any of it.

"It's good to see you again, Sydney," Malik said, his voice caressing her name so sweetly. The way he'd caressed her body. The way she wanted him to caress her body again.

"I bought a ticket," she blurted. Oh, God, where did that come from? Why had she said that? But her brain was refusing to function right. He was here, and she wanted to tell him everything, wanted to spill all her secrets and feelings and hope he felt the same.

He looked puzzled. "A ticket?"

She closed her eyes briefly. Clutched her briefcase. She needed something solid, something to remind her this was real. "To Jahfar," she said, feeling embarrassed and stupid and ridiculous all at once. "I leave tonight."

"Ah, I see. That will be a shame."

"A shame?"

He reached out, his fingers ghosting over her cheek. She tried to lean into the caress, but it was too fleeting to do so. "I had hoped you would attend a party with me."

"A party?" She looked down at her clothes. "I—I'm not dressed for a party."

"I took the liberty of picking something out for you," he said softly.

Sydney swallowed. This was crazy. Nothing made sense, and once more he wasn't saying anything she understood. A party?

"What kind of party is it?" she asked, her throat aching with all she wanted to say. All she didn't know how to say.

"It's for us. It's a celebration."

Her pulse tripped along at the speed of light. If she

kept feeling so many emotions, she was going to explode from the strain. "What are we celebrating?"

He smiled, and her belly lurched. Then he slipped an arm around her, pulled her in close. She tilted her head back to look up at him. Her grip on the briefcase loosened as he took it in one hand and tossed it onto a chair.

His sensual lips curved. "I know it is presumptuous of me, but I had hoped we could celebrate our marriage. Our lives together. Our happiness."

A tear slipped down her cheek. "Malik—"

He put a finger over her lips. His heat seared her. Her body responded to his touch as if it had been starved for him. She felt liquid inside, fluid. Hot.

"Let me speak. This is hard for me, *habibti*. I am not accustomed to speaking of feelings." His golden skin flushed, a muscle in his cheek jumping. But his eyes…his eyes were filled with things she'd never noticed before.

"Words are cheap. Words are meaningless. And yet I know there is value in them, when they are sincere. I've heard many cheap, meaningless words in my life. It has made me immune to words, perhaps. To my detriment, at least where you are concerned."

He drew in a sharp breath. "I did not say what I should have said to you, and I have regretted that. I should have told you that my world went dark when you left it a year ago. That my pride kept me from coming after you when I should have. That I let too much time pass because I kept hoping you would come back to me. How could you not come back to me? I am Prince Malik Al Dhakir."

He was mocking himself. She put a hand over his mouth to stop him. She didn't like hearing him speak that way. "Don't, Malik. Don't berate yourself. We've both done stupid things. I should have never run the way I did. I was a child, as you said. I was impulsive and stupid."

He smiled then. "I like you when you're impulsive."

"How could you? I behaved like an idiot."

"But you also married me in one of those impulsive moments. Unless, of course, you think that was a stupid move. And I wouldn't blame you if you did."

She shook her head. Then she looked down, at where her palms rested on his lapels. The fabric of his tux was soft, expensive. He smelled expensive, looked expensive. So regal, so handsome.

And she was so plain. Plain Sydney Reed.

He tilted her chin up. "Stop that, Sydney."

"Stop what?"

"Thinking you aren't good enough."

"That's not what I was thinking." But she was, of course. She dropped her forehead to his chest. "I'm working on it, Malik. It's a lifetime habit and I can't change it overnight."

"Listen to me, Sydney." She looked up again, her breath catching at the intensity in his gaze. "You are the finest person I know. The kindest, gentlest and least selfish. I want to be with you. I want you in my life, today and always. But it won't always be easy. You have met my mother. She will not change her mind about you, but know that I don't care. I only ever cared for the way you would feel to know this, not because I was embarrassed or ashamed or regretful of *you*."

Everything he said made her heart swell. "Your mother doesn't bother me. So long as you want me, I could care less what she thinks." She bit her lip. "You do want me, right? You want to be married to me?"

He looked slightly exasperated. "Have I not said this?"

Sydney laughed softly. "I'm just double-checking."

"What is there to check? I have told you how I feel, what I want. What I have always wanted."

She reached up and ran her fingers along his jaw. There was more she needed to know, though it didn't change the way she felt about him. "Why did you marry me, Malik? Was it to get out of another arranged marriage? Was I the most convenient choice? Or was it something more?"

He looked suddenly fierce. The breeze whipped up then, ruffling his hair. She ached to smooth it, but did not do so.

"I did not want to marry my mother's choice, no. But I am far too old for her to truly be able to force me to do something I do not want."

"But your brother—"

"Even a king cannot force a marriage if both parties do not agree."

She felt as if a great weight had been lifted, as if there were no longer anything holding her down and she would fly away on a current of joy and happiness if Malik did not keep his arms around her.

"I love you, Malik. That's what I was coming to Jahfar to say. And I know you care for me. I know because of the things you do, not because of the words you say. I completely understand now."

"I'm not quite sure you do," he said softly. "But I intend to show you." And then he bent and kissed her, his mouth hot and possessive and so sexy it hurt.

She wound her arms around him, arched into him, her body greedy for him. He held her hard, tilting her head back as he kissed her so thoroughly she knew she would never be the same again. She wanted to rip his tuxedo off, get to the golden skin and smooth muscles beneath. She wanted to work her way down his body, take him in her mouth and then work her way back up again.

She wanted him inside her. She wanted to sleep curled up with him, and wake in his arms. She wanted to eat with him, laugh with him, be in the same room with him even if they weren't doing or saying anything.

"Ahem."

Malik squeezed her to him, his tongue delving into her mouth one more time before setting her away from him. Taj stood in the entry, looking resplendent in a tuxedo. He grinned, a brow arching in good humor.

"So you have decided to forgive my idiot brother, Sydney? This is very good, as he would have been embarrassed to arrive at the party alone."

"Taj," Malik warned.

Sydney laughed. "I think there are two idiots here, but yes, we're going to the party together."

"Wonderful," Taj said. "Then shall we move along? Sydney needs to change, and our chariot awaits."

CHAPTER FIFTEEN

EVERYTHING went perfectly, though perhaps it should not have. Malik was very aware that he'd not said quite everything to her that he needed to say. He was still choking when it came to baring his heart, to stripping it raw and giving her the power to slay him.

He'd told her the truth, that he needed her and desired her and that his life was hell without her. But that wasn't the extent of it. It was more than that. Deeper and more beautiful than he'd ever imagined.

He was a headstrong man. It had taken him far too long to admit to himself just why he needed her in his life. He'd been in love with her almost from the beginning. Not from the first moment, of course. Then he'd only wanted to get her naked. He didn't apologize for it.

But somewhere along the way, she'd become vital to him. He'd known it deep down, even while he'd talked himself into thinking that he enjoyed her company and wanted her with him because she didn't demand anything from him.

She'd been fresh and innocent in a way he'd never been, and he'd been drawn to her. From the first moment they made love, he'd felt the connection to her. She had felt it, too. That's what had made them both so reckless.

He'd feared losing her, so he'd married her. And she had feared losing him, so she ran away when she thought she might. What a pair they made.

He watched her across the room. She was so beautiful and vibrant. She glowed with life and happiness. He'd thought, when he'd let her go in the desert, that he would never see her again.

She looked up and caught his eye, smiled that smile that drove him crazy for her. It was as if she smiled only for him, her eyes lighting, her entire face glowing with love.

Love. It was real, her love. He'd never been loved before, but now that he had, he wasn't ever letting a day go by without rejoicing in that love. Basking in it.

His eyes skimmed over her, over the claret silk dress he'd picked. It was strapless, skimming her curves like a lover, glimmering like the stars on a clear desert night. She'd pinned her hair up, revealing the graceful column of her neck. Driving him wild.

He wanted to bite her. Gently, teasingly, making her moan and beg while he primed her body with his mouth and hands.

The hotel he'd chosen for the party was very exclusive, very *riche*. Their guests ate hors d'oeuvres, sipped champagne and laughed like they were having a good time. Soft light illuminated the room, caressed the form of the woman he loved. He couldn't take his eyes off her. Sydney stood near her sister, her arm looped in Alicia's, smiling at something the gentleman talking to them said.

A hard rush of anger filled him when he thought of what Sydney had told him about her sister's boyfriend. Malik had already made a call. Jeffrey Orr would never bother Alicia again. As much as it disgusted Malik to do so, he'd made sure the man got a job transfer he couldn't refuse. He should be in the bottom of a prison cell, but instead he was getting a pay raise in a new location halfway around the world.

Malik would keep tabs on him, though. If he tried to harm another woman, he would find himself in the bottom of a cell. Because the country he was going to was a lot more intolerant than this one.

Sydney looked up and caught his eye. Her smile made him ache. It *was* only for him, he realized, that soft curve of the lips that said how much she wanted him. Needed him.

Loved him.

God, he was a lucky man.

She gave her sister a squeeze and then made her way over to him. He worked to smooth his expression, his emotions roiling inside as if he were a green boy who'd never been with a woman. He wanted her desperately, and he wanted her to know what he'd done to protect her sister. Thinking of Alicia made him angry all over again.

"What's wrong, Malik? You look as if you could chew nails."

He slipped an arm around her, anchored her to him as he dipped his head to kiss her. He would never tire of showing off his beautiful wife. "It is nothing. A business deal."

He wouldn't spoil the atmosphere of their party, but he would tell her later when they were alone. He didn't think she would be angry at what he'd done, but he couldn't be sure. And yet he would do the same thing again. No man should treat a woman the way Jeffrey Orr had treated Alicia. If he'd been Jahfaran, the punishment would have been infinitely swifter.

"You were very sneaky," she said, smiling up at him. "I had no idea you were even in town. Alicia and my parents kept the secret quite well."

"They love you very much. They are proud of you."

"For what? For getting a rich and handsome husband?" She was teasing him, but he was deadly serious.

"No. For being who you are, Sydney."

He could tell she didn't quite believe it, but he would have a lifetime to convince her of how amazing she was. She would believe it eventually, just as he'd learned to believe he was deserving of love.

Her eyes sparkled in the soft light and he knew she was holding back tears. "I tried to call you."

"I'm sorry," he said. "By the time I realized I'd missed your calls, I was here and the plans were in motion."

"You could have called me," she said.

He squeezed her to him. "No, I could not. I don't do well over the phone, as you very well know."

She rolled her eyes. "Oh, Malik, you have to learn sometime. It's not all that hard."

"Maybe it is," he murmured in her ear. "Maybe it's *very* hard."

Her breath drew in sharply. "Do you think it would be scandalous if we left now?"

He made a show of checking his watch. As if he weren't dying to get her alone as well. As if he had all the time in the world.

"I think we can safely go home now," he said.

She grinned up at him, and his breath caught. How had he ever allowed her to leave him? How had he lived even a moment without her?

He lowered his head and kissed her. He intended

it to be brief, but the instant their mouths touched, it
was like setting a match to a fuse. She was soft, warm,
delicious. His tongue delved into the recesses of her
mouth, claimed her boldly and completely. She was
his. Forever.

The sound of cheering and clapping brought him
back to reality. He broke the kiss, more annoyed than
anything.

Sydney ducked her head against him, her cheeks
turning scarlet. "I think we should go *now*."

Malik laughed. "And so we shall."

He bade everyone a good night before leading Sydney to the waiting limo. They were suddenly very quiet
as the limo pulled away from the hotel. She moved to
the other side of the car and he kept his place near the
door. If he touched her in the darkened interior, they
would go up in flame.

And he wanted to do this right. He wanted a bed,
flowers, candles, champagne. He wanted everything
to be perfect for her.

"I'd ask why you're staying over there," she said, her
soft voice cutting into the night. "But I think I know."

"I'm only a man, Sydney. I can only handle so much
before I snap."

She purred in the darkness, and he hardened instantly. "I can't *wait* for you to snap."

When they finally reached their destination, she
looked at him wonderingly. The Malibu house gleamed
in the moonlight as the limo came to a stop in the circular drive, its engine still humming quietly.

"It seemed appropriate," he said with a shrug. "It
is where we began this journey the second time. I am
quite fond of it."

They didn't make it to the bedroom. As soon as the front door closed behind them, they were in each other's arms, kissing, touching, removing clothes, revealing their bodies as they revealed their souls to one another.

Malik wanted to worship her properly, but everything seemed to go too fast. In no time, he was carrying her to the couch and laying her on it as she shifted her hips up to him and pleaded with him to end her torment.

"We need to slow down," he said. Panted, really.

"No, no, I don't want to."

She wrapped her legs around him, her heels in his buttocks. He hesitated, wanting to remember this moment, the rightness of it. The way she looked as she lay beneath him naked, her nipples still glistening from his mouth, her lips swollen from his kisses. Her hair wild and free, tumbling down her back in a riot of flame.

Beautiful. *His.*

"Malik, please," she said. "Stop teasing me."

And that was it. He surrendered. Utterly and completely. Malik lifted her to him and drove into her molten heat.

Bliss. Comfort. Rightness.

Love.

Sydney had never been so happy in her life. She lay wrapped in Malik's arms, her body spent, her heart full. They'd found their way to the bed, but not before he'd opened the sliding glass doors to the outside. A soft breeze from the ocean whispered over them. It wasn't cool, not after they'd been so incandescently hot together, but it was welcome.

The ocean crashed on the beach below, the waves eternal and endless. She'd thought of Malik as a wave, a relentless wave dragging her below the surface.

She'd been wrong.

He was relentless, but he wasn't dragging her down. He was lifting her up, asking her to accompany him. To be by his side always.

She could do that. She intended to do that.

She turned in his arms, saw that he was awake. Watching her. Her heart did that little flip it always did when he was near.

"What are you thinking?" she asked, tracing his lip with her thumb. It hurt to love him so much, but she would learn how to live with the pain. It was a good pain to have.

"I am thinking there are no words to describe this moment with you. But I have to say the best ones I have, because they will come the closest to it."

Sydney ran her hand over his chest, up into his hair. She loved touching him. Could never get enough of touching him. "Then they will be perfect, Malik. Because I know you would not use them otherwise."

His white teeth flashed in the darkness. "Then I shall say them."

He turned her onto her back, rose above her on an elbow and traced the line of her collarbone. Her skin tingled with pleasure. Though she should be burnt out by now, tongues of flame licked her from the inside out. How very quickly she wanted him again.

She put a hand on his chest, felt the hard beat of his heart.

"I love you Sydney. You made me believe in love when I didn't think I ever would. And though I fear the words are not adequate, I love you."

"Oh, Malik," she said through a haze of tears, her heart squeezing tight. "They are perfect."

"I am still, however, a proponent of action," he said, dipping his head to suckle her nipple into his mouth.

"Oh, yes," she gasped, clasping his head to her as her body spiraled higher. "So am I…"

* * * * *

#3117 IN THE HEAT OF THE SPOTLIGHT
The Bryants: Powerful & Proud
Kate Hewitt
Ambitious tycoon Luke Bryant's power and passion
will lay scandalous Aurelie bare.... She's determined
not to let him get beneath her skin, but faced with
the sexiest man she's ever met, Aurelie can't resist
just one touch!

#3118 NO MORE SWEET SURRENDER
Scandal in the Spotlight
Caitlin Crews
Ivan Korovin's only solution to a PR nightmare
created by outspoken Miranda Sweet is to give the
ravenous public what they want—to see these two
enemies become lovers! But soon the mutually
beneficial charade becomes too hot to handle!

#3119 PRIDE AFTER HER FALL
Lucy Ellis
Lorelai is an heiress on the edge, hiding her
desperation behind her glossy blond hair and even
brighter smile. Legendary racing driver Nash Blue
never could resist a challenge—and he begins his
biggest yet: unwrapping the real Lorelai St James....

#3120 LIVING THE CHARADE
Michelle Conder
When buttoned-up Miller Jacob needs to find a fake
boyfriend, Valentino Ventura, maverick of the racing
world, is the last person she wants. Up for the job,
Valentino can't wait to help Miller let her hair—and
whatever else she wants—down!

You can find more information on upcoming Harlequin®
titles, free excerpts and more at www.Harlequin.com.

EXPHPCNM0113RB

REQUEST YOUR FREE BOOKS!

2 FREE NOVELS PLUS
2 FREE GIFTS!

YES! Please send me 2 FREE Harlequin Presents® novels and my 2 FREE gifts (gifts are worth about $10). After receiving them, if I don't wish to receive any more books, I can return the shipping statement marked "cancel." If I don't cancel, I will receive 6 brand-new novels every month and be billed just $4.30 per book in the U.S. or $4.99 per book in Canada. That's a saving of at least 14% off the cover price! It's quite a bargain! Shipping and handling is just 50¢ per book in the U.S. and 75¢ per book in Canada.* I understand that accepting the 2 free books and gifts places me under no obligation to buy anything. I can always return a shipment and cancel at any time. Even if I never buy another book, the two free books and gifts are mine to keep forever.

106/306 HDN FERQ

Name	(PLEASE PRINT)

Address	Apt. #

City	State/Prov.	Zip/Postal Code

Signature (if under 18, a parent or guardian must sign)

HARLEQUIN *Presents*®

The truth is more shocking than the headlines!

Having been at war on the front pages for months,
the world holds its breath waiting to see what
happens when two enemies meet. Media darling
Miranda Sweet refuses to have her career ruined by a
very unplanned—scorching—kiss from martial arts
celebrity Ivan Korovin. Their kiss may have gone
viral...but the *real* scandal has only just begun.

NO MORE SWEET
SURRENDER

by *USA TODAY* bestselling author

Caitlin Crews

Pick up a copy January 22, 2013.